Logan's
LUCK

Logan's
LUCK

BY

LEXI POST

Logan's Luck

Last Chance Series Book #4

For information contact Lexi Post at www.lexipostbooks.com.

Cover design by Bella Media Management
Cover photo: Cover Me Photography by Becky McGraw
Cover model: Jose Ruiz
Cover background photo: Robert A. Fabich Sr.
Formatting by Bella Media Management

Print ISBN: 978-0-9985260-4-1

Excerpt of *Cowboys Match* Copyright © 2015 by Lexi Post

LOGAN'S LUCK
Last Chance Series, Book 4

By Lexi Post

Logan Williams has plenty of luck. The problem is, it's all bad.

Logan Williams is not happy his cousin retained the services of Dr. Jenna for the Last Chance Ranch. She may be the local vet, but he'd hoped never to see her again. It had taken too long to forget her the first time.

Jenna Atkins is not afraid of Logan's bark because any man who looks at his baby daughter the way he does, must have a good heart buried somewhere in there. That doesn't mean she plans to get any closer than they already were.

But when baby Charlotte's mother arrives and sets her sights on Logan, Jenna discovers a territorial side of herself she didn't know she had. The question is, should she walk away and let Logan's luck run its course or should she interfere? Knowing Logan, either way, she's bound to get hurt.

Acknowledgments

For Bob Fabich, Sr., an amazing husband and a wonderful father. And for my sister Paige Wood, who is always there when I need her.

A special thank you to Misty Dawn for giving me the name for Butterball.

I have the most awesome readers! To that end, I want to thank readers Tracy Jacobs and Cary Comas for loving my books, and a shout out to reader Sioban Muir who is a great author in her own right!

As usual, Marie Patrick, my awesome friend and critique partner kept me on the straight and narrow and supported me when life got in the way on this one.

Lastly, thank you to Pamela Todd and KC Crocker for arranging their schedules so they could give this story a final look over. You two rock!

Author's Note

Logan's Luck was inspired by Bret Harte's short story, "The Luck of Roaring Camp," first published sometime between 1868 and 1872. In Harte's story, a baby is born to a whore in a mining camp of all men. When the baby's mother dies, the men designate one person to take care of the newborn.

Though the baby is named Tommy, he is referred to as "The Luck." The camp's luck soon takes a turn for the better when Tommy is born, and that summer gold is found in high quantities. Unfortunately, at the end of winter as the snow melts in the high mountains of the Sierras, the camp's luck turns bad. The North Fork leaps over its banks and floods the valley of Roaring Camp, taking some of the cabins and men with it. They find one of the men near death still holding The Luck in his arms. When the other men check the baby, they find it has passed and the man that holds him soon follows, saying "Tell the boys I've got The Luck with me now."

What would it be like for a baby to grow up among so many men? Would their rough ways be put in check? Would they band together to raise it and protect it? And what would happen if a woman wanted a say in the baby's upbringing? Or worse yet, two women? Would the father welcome the feminine touch or would it depend on the woman?

Chapter One

"What the hell is she doing here?" Logan Williams looked up from where he knelt on the barn floor to scowl at the local vet.

His brother stepped up next to her. "Dr. Jenna's here to help."

He glared at Trace. "I don't remember asking for any help."

"You never do. Maybe if you did, life would go a little smoother for you." He grinned. "Now, no fighting while I'm gone." Trace winked then turned on his heel and strode out of the barn whistling.

Damn troublemaker. It was just his luck that when he moved to the Last Chance horse rescue ranch, his extended family had retained the services of Dr. Jenna Atkins, local vet and former one-night-stand. She was the only woman he'd fought the urge to call for a month before their night together was finally put to rest where it belonged. "Well, since you're here, you might as well make yourself useful. Go to the house and get me a couple bottled waters. This is going to be a while."

The five-foot four-inch woman in a white button down collared shirt and snug blue jeans crossed her arms over her bountiful chest. Her blue-green eyes sent need spiraling up his spine, despite the anger in them. "Let's reverse that, shall we? Since I'm the medically trained vet," she lifted her large leather bag of medicines and equipment, "I suggest you go get *us* some waters and I'll take mama's vitals. What's her name?"

He ground his teeth at her logic, trying to find a way around it. He couldn't. "Her name is Macy."

Jenna opened the stall door and walked in crooning to the horse, who, damn her, nickered at the vet. Jenna stood right next to him and set her bag on the concrete floor. "You're in my way."

Swallowing a completely inappropriate response, he rose to his feet, purposefully towering over her. "I'll be right back." His words came out like a threat, but he didn't care. Brushing by her, he exited the stall and stalked out of the barn.

Thoroughly pissed off, he swore if he ran in to Trace he would lay him out cold. Ignoring the final reds and purples in the darkening sky, he took the three steps to the porch and threw open the front door. The screen banged against the doorframe as he stalked down the hall to the kitchen.

When he stepped into the room, he halted at his grandmother's scowl. "Don't you go slamming my doors. How old are you? Thirteen?"

It wasn't his grandmother's scolding that calmed him so much as it was his sleeping fifteen-month old daughter in his grandmother's arms. "She's getting too big for that, Gram. Here, let me put her in our room."

She looked down at his daughter and her scowl faded. Charlotte had that effect on everyone who helped out at the ranch. Despite how rambunctious she was while awake, everyone doted on her.

When she slept, you'd think she was the Queen of Sheba the way they all tiptoed around the ranch house. The thing was, Charlotte was as likely to sleep at mid-afternoon as at night, her schedule like that of a puppy, which unfortunately, gave him little sleep. Luckily, the night sleeping had improved.

2

"She'll never be too big for my arms." His grandmother practically crooned her words.

"Come on, Gram. I bet your left arm is completely numb now. Let me take her up."

His grandmother nodded, and he lifted his daughter into his arms. As he turned away to head upstairs, he caught his grandmother in his peripheral vision, shaking out her arm.

He didn't say anything as he turned the corner and climbed the stairs. Everyone in the house, which luckily was just his grandparents and himself now, doted on his daughter.

When he'd first arrived, a new single dad without a home, the place was bursting at the seams with Cole and old Billy, not to mention Cole's now wife Lacey. Since his cousin, Cole, jointly owned the horse rescue ranch with their grandparents, Logan really couldn't say anything. Then his brother Trace had shown up during his divorce and getting sleep had been more a wish than a reality.

At the top of the stairs, he turned left and brought Charlotte into his room with the two twin beds. Next to one of them was Charlotte's crib. There was an empty room across the hall, now that everyone had moved out, but he wasn't quite ready to have his daughter that far away from him. The small bedroom at the end of the hall his grandfather was renovating, so it was unusable.

Gently, he laid Charlotte down, her little hand still holding her teddy with the cowboy hat. His grandmother had insisted that she have a horse as soon as she could crawl, even if it was a stuffed one, but that animal remained in the crib all day while the teddy went everywhere.

He gazed down at his daughter, still amazed that she was really his. Despite all his precautions, all his maneuverers to avoid any kind of entanglement with a woman beyond a quick night of sex, something had failed. At first, he thought it was just more of his perpetual bad luck, but having Charlotte in his life had changed everything...except his luck.

He brushed her thick brown hair, kept short after she started chewing on it. He'd had to cut his own hair short after she pulled it one too many times, leaving sticky syrup in it that would have taken days to wash out.

He still didn't know anything about being a dad. All he had to go on was what he remembered with his own father, who he admired most of his life...until the end just before he passed. That's when his bad luck had really started.

Thanks to his grandparents though, he was learning a lot more about being a parent and especially about being a parent of a little girl. Hopefully, she'd have better luck and be more successful than he ever was.

Turning away, he gazed at her from the doorway then turned off the light. A little pony nightlight illuminated the floor so he could find his way to his bed once it was dark. He chuckled silently as he descended the stairs. He would have been mortified if his mother had put a nightlight of any kind in his bedroom when he was a boy. He'd been tough, but Charlotte was soft and sweet.

Entering the kitchen, he found his grandmother had moved to another room, so he opened the fridge, grabbed four bottled waters and headed back outside. He wasn't about to tell Jenna, but he was worried about Macy.

When he approached the stall, he heard Macy whine. Damn, he was right, it wasn't going well. He set the water bottles on a beam and leaned over the stall door, in no hurry to get into such a confined space with Jenna. "What's wrong?"

She didn't look at him. "The foal's legs are both coming out at the same time. That won't work. We need to get her up and walking or you could lose both of them."

"Fuck." He pulled open the stall door, his aversion to Jenna forgotten in his concern for Macy.

"Help me get her up."

"Up? She's trying to give birth." He looked at the small legs sticking out the vulva. "If we get her up, the foal might fall back in."

Jenna finally gave him her undivided attention. "That's what I'm hoping."

"What?"

"Listen, if we don't get her up and walking around, you're going to have one dead foal and one sick mama. Darn it, I wish I had Whisper here. At least she'd help instead of question everything I say."

He'd been about to argue, but at her last comment he shut his mouth and moved toward the horse. His brother's girlfriend, Whisper, was amazing with animals, but she was a bit odd. That Jenna would prefer her over himself irritated him, motivating him to show he could help.

With a few coaxing words and a push in the right direction, they got Macy up on her feet again. As he expected, the foal's feet disappeared into Macy.

"Now we need to walk her." Jenna issued orders like she was born to it, which rankled. He was the one who had run a ranch before. *Yeah, and what a mess that was.*

Swallowing his pride, he grabbed a halter. He hoped she knew what she was doing. He'd only had one mare in his lifetime have a difficult birth and they had lost the baby. At the time, it was all they could do to save the mother. Now, he couldn't imagine losing the foal. Must have something to do with being a parent himself.

Jenna walked Macy down to the opening of the barn and back a few times, then she handed him the leads. "Hold those for a moment."

He did as instructed, determined not to say a word. If he did, it wouldn't be helpful, of that he was sure. His gut felt like a bull dozer ran through it.

Jenna moved her hands over Macy's enlarged abdomen then she looked up at him. "Lead her into the stall. I think the foal has moved and Macy is not going to wait much longer. I just hope it has moved enough."

He led Macy inside to the fresh hay he'd put down when he'd noticed her condition. Quickly, he removed the halter. "Okay, Macy. It's up to you now, girl. Don't let me down."

Macy stood still as they backed away, then slowly lowered herself to the floor of the stall again and rolled on to her side. She started to breathe heavy and then the contractions began.

"Here we go. Cross your fingers, pray, or just hope that the foal exits correctly this time, or I will have to perform a cesarean in not so sterile conditions."

"Can't you do something to increase the odds in her favor?" She was a vet after all. "Like drugs or something?"

She frowned at him but turned her attention back to Macy when the horse whined. She spoke quietly. "Do me a favor and stay out of the way."

He ground his teeth to hold in his response. For Macy's sake, he'd step back, but after this, the woman would be getting an earful of opinion from him whether she wanted it or not.

The first hoof appeared enveloped in the white birthing sac. That was a good sign. Another couple heaves on Macy's part and another foot appeared slightly behind the first. *Yes! Come on, Macy!* The next part was critical. *Come on girl. Let's see the head.*

Logan gripped the top of the stall door, his heart beating as if he'd just galloped across the valley and back. He must be getting too old for this because he'd never been this tense with a birth when growing up on his family's ranch.

The mare chuffed and whined as two more contractions hit her. They were very rhythmic so that was good, but he glanced at Jenna and the concern on her face made him want to yell.

Another two heaves of the mare's sides and more of the white sac slid out onto the new hay. He stepped forward only to find his way blocked by a stiff arm.

"Stay out of my way." Jenna moved past him and with practiced precision, slit the white sac to reveal the foal's head. She delicately cleared the animal's orifices before she stepped away again. At the smile on her face, his entire insides relaxed.

Macy gave another whine and the foal spilled out, except for its hind feet. Jenna glanced over at him and nodded, her lips still curved in the joy of a new birth.

At that moment, in the dimly lit barn, she looked like an angel. Her thick brown hair pulled back away from her face, emphasized the flush of her cheeks and the soft curve of her neck. In her happiness, her blue-green eyes almost sparkled.

It took everything he had inside him to stay where he was and not pull her into his arms and kiss her. She made it worse by walking over to him, keeping herself far from Macy and the new foal, who was not yet completely out of its mom's body but would be soon.

"She should be fine, but I'll check them both in about twenty minutes." She kept her voice low, like she had when they were in bed. "It'd be best if we left them alone right now."

He stared at her. He should open the stall door for her, but if he moved his arm, it would wrap around her of its own accord. He couldn't allow that, but he wanted it so much he couldn't think straight. "Jenna."

His voice was husky with his own need.

Her brows knit together in puzzlement. "What? Do you have something you want to say?"

Yes! I want to tell you I want you so much I'd take you right here in the next stall. Instead, he swallowed hard against his own weakness. "I can take it from here."

She frowned as she pulled the stall door open just far enough to slip out before holding it for him. "We can discuss that once you get out of there."

There was nothing to discuss. He'd lived on a ranch his whole life. He could take care of a new born foal, dammit. *Yeah, but you also lost the ranch, so what does that say about your expertise, smart ass?* He stalked through the opening then spun around to confront her.

She quietly latched the stall door. Without turning to look at him, she strode toward the barn exit.

Oh no, she wasn't getting away that easy. He caught up to her just before she reached the open barn doors and grabbed her arm. "There is nothing to discuss. I'll take care of the foal and Macy."

At her surprised look, he lowered his tone. "I didn't call you."

She pulled her arm away. "No, you didn't. You're not very good at that, are you? Returning calls isn't one of your talents, is it?"

It didn't take a brain surgeon to figure out she was talking about the days after their night together when she called him and he didn't return her calls. When he lived near Catalina, he thought someone like her from out of town would be easier to keep away. Joke was on him. He cracked two of his knuckles against his thigh. "Listen, it's just that—"

"Oh, spare me the excuses. We both know I was just some easy lay for you." She stepped closer to him, staring him down even though she was at least ten inches shorter than him. "For your information, I don't do one-night-stands. There was nothing easy about it for me."

Her blue-green eyes sparked with anger, but that very energy called to him as it had that night. Damn. He grabbed her by the shoulders to push her away, but instead, pulled her toward him, his mouth descending.

"I heard Macy was foaling. How's it going in—" Cole's voice stopped him cold.

What the hell was he doing? He dropped his hands from Jenna and stepped to the side, ignoring the surprise in her face. "It started out sticky, but Dr. Jenna got the mare back on track. They're bonding now."

Cole, still in his fire department t-shirt, looked at him then to Jenna then back again. He must have just come home from his latest shift. What timing.

Logan's cousin frowned before retuning his gaze to Jenna. "Were you leaving? I'd like it if you could check on them in a bit. Could you come inside for a cup of coffee?"

She faced Cole. "I would be happy to if you could switch out that coffee for a beer. It was a little nerve-wracking there for a while."

"Of course, whatever you want." Cole opened his arm toward the ranch house, but after Jenna walked by, he shook his head at Logan before following.

Logan could hear him as they walked away. "I hope Logan didn't get in the way. He can be hardheaded at times and that foal is important..."

He fisted his hands to keep from running after them, mainly because he didn't know if he could keep himself from punching Cole or kissing Jenna. Either action would cause a hell of a lot more clean-up than he was willing to commit to, so instead, he strode outside and around to the side of the barn where Black Jack was housed beneath a roof, but with just a steel pipe fence to keep him in.

The horse snorted and moved toward him.

He felt a certain sympathy for the claustrophobic horse. He certainly understood wanting to remain free. "What do you say we go for a quick ride? Then I'll come back and see how the new foal is doing."

Black Jack lifted his nose over the fence.

Logan shook his head, but stroked the horse on its nose, the white star in the middle impossible to ignore. "If you let me in, we can head out."

The horse nudged him, looking for a treat.

"You have a one-track mind, my friend." Stepping away, he moved to the small shed he'd built against the outside of the barn, next to Black Jack's cover. He hefted the saddle from the bench and grabbed the horse's bridle.

In no time, he had the Quarter Horse ready to ride and jumped up on his back. Though Black Jack wanted to head for the valley, he turned him toward the long dirt road that connected the ranch to civilization. The valley terrain was too rough to risk at night. Black Jack had enough trauma for one lifetime.

He had thought he had too.

Jenna followed Cole to the house. She'd made it appear that she needed a drink after helping Macy, but it was Logan's almost-kiss that had her wanting a beer. He'd rattled her far more than the new foal's malposition had. Animals she understood. People she understood. Logan, she didn't.

As she walked up the steps to the porch, she was thankful he'd disappeared. She didn't want to lose the Benson-Hatcher business, but every time she arrived, if Logan was around, he argued with everything she said. If she didn't know better, she'd think he was afraid of her knowledge, though his concern for the horses was real.

She refused to be intimidated. The horse rescue ranch needed her more than any other client she had and they were quick to pay, especially since Whisper had set-up a trust for the care of the horses. She just had to forget she and Logan had one amazing day and night together.

The house was a bit warmer than the cool September evening. At least the heat of the days dropped below triple digits on occasion now, always a welcome reprieve for native Arizonans like herself.

"I'm sure everyone is anxious to hear the good news." Cole looked back at her as they headed for the kitchen. "We haven't had a baby born here since I turned it into a horse rescue ranch."

She smiled, happy to have another topic to focus on. "The foal shouldn't have any long-term complications from the difficult birth. I'll make sure in a few minutes. I don't want to infringe on the bonding period." And hopefully, Logan wouldn't either.

They turned the corner into the large kitchen. The matriarch of the family, Annette Benson, grandmother to Logan and Trace, and their cousins, Cole and Dillon, greeted her first.

"You must tell us. Do we have a new baby to welcome?" The fit, older woman with pristine white hair pulled back in a ponytail, stood, reaching out her hands in welcome.

Jenna grinned as she took them in her own. "You sure do."

Annette squeezed her hands. "This is wonderful news. Cole, get the lady a drink."

Cole, already at the refrigerator, smirked. "On it."

"Come sit down and relax a bit." Annette pointed at Trace who sat on the other side of the empty high chair. "Give your seat to Jenna. She's worked twice as hard as you today."

Trace laughed as he rose. "Gram, I don't doubt it."

Jenna rolled her eyes at Trace, who since falling for her

odd friend, Whisper, seemed to be in a perpetually good mood. "Thank you."

He bowed before moving around the table to sit opposite her.

Cole handed her a cold beer after first twisting off the cap.

She took a very unladylike gulp then raised it toward him. "Thanks. I needed that."

Annette frowned, resuming her seat. "Was it that difficult?"

Trace answered before she could open her mouth. "Macy wasn't the problem. She had to deal with Logan."

His words hit far too close to home for her to come up with a suitable response. Luckily, she didn't have to.

"That boy." Annette shook her head. "He needs a good kick in the pants."

Surprisingly, Trace came to his brother's defense. "Now, Gram, I think he's probably had a few too many of those already."

"Well, he obviously needs one more."

Not sure what Trace referred to and uncomfortable with the subject, Jenna changed it by addressing Cole. "Where's Lacey?"

Cole's face softened from firefighter/ranch owner to totally smitten husband in a split second. "She's on her way. She and Whisper just got back from Poker Flat."

Jenna swallowed the beer she'd just sipped and raised her eyebrows. "Poker Flat? Lacey took Whisper to the nudist resort?"

Cole grinned and nodded toward his brother.

She turned her head to find Trace frowning. "Yeah. Supposedly, there was a wild burrow there who wouldn't leave one of the guests alone. Followed him everywhere. Lacey said she needed Whisper's help to find out what was wrong with the animal."

Cole laughed. "He thinks it was all a ruse to get Whisper to the resort. My fine cousin here is jealous."

She grinned before taking another swig of her beer. To discover easy-going Trace wasn't happy made her feel appropriately avenged since he enjoyed it just a little too much that she rubbed Logan the wrong way.

Trace grumbled. "Wait until one of the women decide to take Charlotte to Poker Flat, then see who gets pissed."

Annette shook her head. "Being around Lacey and Whisper would be good for her. Maybe she'll discover an interest in music or dance. It's bad enough she's growing up among so many men folk."

Jenna doubted very much that Charlotte would be anything but a tomboy, especially with Logan for a father. She might have a chance at girly hobbies with Lacey, but Whisper was more likely to teach her how to suck the moisture from a cactus than discuss the latest boy band. Whisper probably didn't even know what a boy band was.

Jenna examined the high chair next to her where Charlotte usually sat. When she was younger, she'd had a plan. Go to school, meet the man of her dreams, then on to veterinary school, buy a house, set up practice, and have a baby then two years later have another.

Her entire plan went off track when the man of her dreams turned out to be an avid hunter and her loans from graduate school made it more than difficult to make ends meet.

If it hadn't been for Whisper keeping her truck at Jenna's place and letting her use it when she needed it, she wouldn't have been able to take on the additional ranches she had. Her little sedan couldn't reach some of the ranches thanks to the rough terrain and Monsoon washes.

Lacey and Whisper walked into the kitchen. Cole was

already out of his chair to give his wife a kiss and hug and Trace wasn't far behind.

The love of the Benson-Hatcher-Williams family just accentuated her own loneliness. Even when she was growing up, it had only been the three of them.

"Jenna? Why are you here? Were there problems with the birth? Is Macy okay?" Whisper's usual bluntness didn't bother her in the least.

"There were, but nothing I couldn't handle. Would you like to—"

Heavy footsteps striding down the hallway announced the newest arrival just before Logan's body filled the doorway, a scowl on his face as he scanned them all until he settled on her. "You better check on them now. It's getting late."

She purposefully looked at her watch before taking another sip of beer. She set the empty bottle down before responding. "I was planning to." She moved her gaze to Cole. "I appreciate the beer, but you're still getting a bill."

He chuckled. "Of course. I just hope you don't charge me extra for having to deal with him." He hooked his thumb toward his glowering cousin in the doorway.

She smirked. "Have I yet?"

Cole laughed, and she rose from her chair.

"Thank you for the hospitality, Annette."

The older woman nodded regally. "You're welcome any time. Thank you for helping the latest addition to our family arrive safely."

She smiled before heading for the door.

Logan stepped aside and followed her out. She kept her walk to a stroll despite her growing irritation with the man behind her.

"It's been well over a half hour. I expected you to have checked on them and left by now."

That was it. She spun around and he halted, stepping back as his eyes widened in surprise.

"What the hell do you have against me?" She pointed at him, poking her finger into his hard chest, then wishing she hadn't when the image of his naked pectoral rose inside her brain.

She pulled her hand back as if burned and squinted at him. "Do you think the veterinary school I attended wasn't accredited? Do you question the validity of the degree hanging on my wall? Or is it that I simply wasn't a good enough lay for you?" Ah, damn, she didn't mean to say that part out loud.

Mortified, she ignored his stunned expression and turned, marching across the yard as if she could pound out the humiliation of having revealed her insecurity. When she reached the barn, she softened her steps until she arrived at the stall.

Glancing in at the new baby suckling its mother's teat helped calm her. Silently, but speedily, she ducked into the stall and stepped behind the two. The placenta had still not been expelled. She certainly wasn't going to wait for it, not with Logan around.

Reassured the two horses were bonding, she stepped back into the dimly lit barn to find Logan waiting for her at the entrance. Ignoring him, she packed up her bag and hefted it over her shoulder then strode toward him. Her plan was to brush by him without a word, but his hand shot out and grabbed her arm.

She tried to pull away, but he didn't let go.

"Dammit, Jenna." His voice was husky, like it had been that fateful night when she'd thrown caution to the wind and had fallen for the charming, considerate, cowboy—who turned in to the man before her.

"What?" She tilted her head back to look him in the eye. He was too darn tall and too good-looking.

"I—ah, hell."

His mouth came down on hers so fast, she froze. But as warm tingles trickled across her skin and her muscles weakened, she pushed away, shaking her head at him. "No." It came out choked, almost like a cry and she cleared her throat. "No, I'm not going there again. You burned that bridge, buddy."

He stared at her, but there was no scowl on his face. There was no expression either, or another word.

Ugh, the man was impossible. Hefting her bag from the ground where it had fallen, she stalked away. She tried to get her heart rate to slow, but her breath was still coming too quickly. When she reached her car, she threw her bag in the back and jumped inside, locking the doors to keep him out and her in.

As soon as the car revved to life, she backed out only to see Logan still standing there watching her. Darn, she forgot to tell him to call her if the mare had trouble with the placenta. Screw it. She'd call Cole when she got home. Hopefully, Logan also knew about the umbilical cord, but she'd remind Cole anyway. He might not live in the main house anymore, but he could pass the word on to Logan.

Hitting the gas, she drove down the long dirt driveway, watching for animals in her headlights, refusing to look in the rearview mirror again until a second curve made it absolutely impossible to see him.

Once she turned onto the paved two-lane highway headed toward Wickenburg, she finally gave in to the turmoil inside her heart, angrily wiping away the tears in her eyes.

She didn't cry for what could have been with the man who kept their relationship to a one-night-stand. That was her fault for falling in love with him after no more than a day at the fair and a night of amazing lovemaking.

Nope, she cried for herself because as long as he kept a piece of her heart with him, she would never find someone else, and she was sick and tired of being alone.

Chapter Two

Logan pulled the diaper under Charlotte's rump as she reached out to him with her favorite teddy bear. "Da-da, mine."

He grinned and fastened the tabs on each side. "You bettcha, Sunshine. I'm all yours."

She giggled and promptly stuck the teddy's bear's hat in her mouth, her version of kisses. Whipping it out again, she held it up toward him.

Instead of kissing the slobbered-on teddy, he picked her up and carried her to the dresser. With one hand, he pulled open the top drawer. "What do you want to wear today?"

She pushed the teddy against his cheek. "Kissie." She pulled it back and slapped it against his cheek. "Kissie, Da-da."

He grabbed up a pink striped shirt and purple pants with pink butterflies on them before closing the drawer with his hip and walking to his bed.

"Da-da!" Charlotte smacked the teddy against his chest. "Kissie! Da-da!"

He dropped the clothes on the quilt then plopped his daughter on her back on the bed. "You want kisses? I'll give you kisses." He lowered his head and kissed her belly.

18

Squeals of laughter filled their room and his heart thrummed with joy. She was his reason for being. After a couple of wet kisses to her belly, he raised his head. "You want more kisses from Daddy?"

Charlotte's green eyes sparkled with mischief. She thrust the teddy at him. "Da-da kissies!"

He laughed. "You little scamp." Pushing her arm aside with his face, he kissed her little belly all over, much to her delight. Her skin was so soft, he was careful not to scratch it with his still unshaven chin.

"You're going to spoil her." His Gram's voice didn't deter him at all.

He lifted Charlotte high into the air before setting her back on the bed. "She deserves to be spoiled."

His daughter dropped her teddy and lifted her hands. "Up. Up."

He scooped up the shirt, quickly inserted her arms and pulled it over her head. Charlotte's eyebrows lowered as her hand found her teddy bear and she threw it over the side of the bed.

His gram laughed. "You're going to have your hands full."

Grabbing up the pants, he spared a glance toward the door. His grandmother leaned against the frame, her arms crossed and a warm smile on her face. He gave her a quick eye roll before kneeling down and capturing his daughter's flailing legs.

"Up. Up. Da-da, up!"

"Let me get your pants on and I'll bring you up."

She stopped moving for a few seconds as she pondered his words. He didn't kid himself that she understood that yet.

He'd just finished getting the pants over her diaper when she decided she had to rollover and wiggle off the bed.

He let her go, his anticipation cutting off his breath.

With one hand on the bed, she toddled along it until she couldn't hold on any longer, but the teddy was still too far to reach. As soon as she took one step away, she wobbled and fell back on her butt. Undaunted, she crawled to her teddy and picked it up, rolling over into a sitting position to hold up her hands again. "Up."

"I thought she was going to do it this time." His grandmother sighed. "But better not to rush it. Once she's walking on her own, she'll be impossible to keep track of, mark my words."

He picked up his daughter and swung her up in the air, her laughter wiping out his disappointment. "I know. I just hope she isn't too far behind the curve." He brought her back into his arms and returned to the dresser where he pulled out a pair of tiny white socks.

Charlotte wiggled to get out of his arms. "No. Mimi."

"I think I'm being paged." Gram walked into the room and sat on the other bed. "Here, give her to me. I'll hold squirmy while you put on those socks."

"Thanks." Logan readjusted his hold on his daughter and brought her over. "Here you go."

Charlotte held up the teddy bear as he knelt to put her socks on.

"Mimi, kissie."

His hard as nails grandmother lowered her head and made a big production of kissing the teddy bear. Charlotte giggled.

When he finished pulling on the socks, Gram picked up his daughter. "Come on, sweetie. Time to let your daddy get dressed and out to work. Would you like cereal or toast this morning?"

"Toast. Toast. Toast. Toast…"

The litany continued as Gram brought Charlotte downstairs. His time with his daughter every morning was the best part of the day. It always went downhill from there.

Sighing, he headed for the bathroom and a quick shower. He preferred to sleep nude, but ever since Charlotte came into his life, he'd purchased a half dozen pair of pajama bottoms, one of many adjustments he'd had to make for her, but she was well worth it.

In no time he was showered, dressed, and headed out to the barn. A new load of hay was expected and he wanted to pull the few old bales out. It was easy to concentrate on work with Charlotte happily playing in her playpen under Gram's watchful eye.

He entered the barn to find his brother already there. "I didn't see your truck. Did you ride down?"

Trace turned away from Macy's stall. "Yes. Lightyear needed a good run and Whisper needed my truck to go in to town since hers is still at Dr. Jenna's house. Whisper said she needed to pick up a couple bottles of antibiotics for a wounded cougar hanging around our place."

Logan halted before his brother. "Don't tell me she's putting cream on a cougar."

Trace chuckled. "Not that she would hesitate to, but no, she's mixing it into food she leaves out at night. Must be working because every night the food is gone, and we still see the cougar outside our firelight."

"How do you know some coyote isn't eating it, and the cougar isn't just waiting for you to fall asleep and the fire to go out?"

Trace had picked up a small cooler, but he stilled and looked sideways at him. "Because Whisper says it's helping."

"Right." Logan shook his head before turning to view the new foal. He'd had a late night taking care of the afterbirth and making sure everything continued to go well between the two. As much as he hated to admit it, if Jenna hadn't had Cole remind him about the betadine for the umbilical cord, he'd have completely forgotten. It had been that long since he'd had a mare foal. His family had had a cattle ranch like his grandparents, not a horse rescue ranch like the one Cole had created.

The foal was a male. He lay next to Macy as she licked his face. Pleased with their progress, Logan moved away and donned a pair of work gloves.

Trace took a swallow from a bottle of water before stuffing it back in his cooler. "Cole said he'd be here when the truck arrived."

Logan climbed up the ladder to the hayloft. "Good. With three of us, we just might get this done before lunch." He strode toward the hay bales against the back wall and hefted one in each hand. "Hope you have your gloves on because here they come." He dropped the bales over the edge to the floor below.

An unexpected shuffle and bleat came from Macy's stall. He walked along the loft until he could see the pair. The foal stood where he'd been lying just moments ago. This wasn't going to work. The haybales hitting the barn floor were nothing compared to the sound of the fork lift.

Striding back to the ladder, he descended before meeting Trace as he was about to re-enter the barn after lugging the bales outside. "We can't do this with Macy and the foal in there. Just the sound of the haybale startled it. If we use the forklift..."

Trace nodded. He'd owned a horse ranch before losing it through his divorce. "We have two choices. Either we lug every bale up into the loft by hand, or we move Macy and her baby. What did you name it?"

"Charlotte's Horse for now. Is it safe to move them so soon?"

Trace nodded. "From what I saw, I'd say yes. A lot better than leaving them in here. We could bring them to the corral just south of the barn. That one still has the shelter we set up for when the youth group visited."

That corral was not too far, but hopefully, far enough. "Can you get the last of the old bales out of there?" He hooked his thumb toward the barn. "I want to add a little more protection to that shelter. It's just a roof, but we have those boards I bought for Black Jack's shelter that he didn't want."

Trace chuckled. "No, he didn't want them. How many did he bust?"

Logan frowned. "It only took two before I listened to him. He's a stubborn horse. Good thing he's here."

"Good thing he's yours." Trace smirked. "Sure, I'll haul the rest of the bales out. Go ahead, but make it fast. That hay truck is due here any minute."

"Thanks." He headed to the shed on the other side of the barn and quickly loaded the ATV trailer with wood.

~~*~~

Jenna pulled up to the ranch house at Last Chance and cut the engine. She could think of a hundred other tasks she needed to attend to, but Macy and the foal had to be her top priority, no matter how little sleep she'd had thanks to a certain cowboy living here.

Falling asleep had been easy. Staying asleep while her dreams were riddled with the memory of Logan's kiss last night and their time together over a year ago had been impossible.

She glanced at herself in her rearview mirror. Great. She looked like she felt. What did that matter? She was a vet and she had a job to do. Unclipping her hair, she wound it around and folded it under then reclipped it. Good enough. It wasn't as if she wanted to impress anyone.

Grabbing her bag from the passenger seat, she stepped out

then headed for the barn. The noise coming from inside had her quickening her steps. A glance at the huge truck with half the hay missing told her exactly what was going on.

Darn it. There was a new foal inside. Was Logan totally clueless? She stalked to the entrance and froze.

Cole sat in the fork lift, lowering the fork to the ground, but above in the hayloft Trace and Logan worked on either side of the hay bales, stacking them toward the back. Both men were shirtless, but from her spot, she could only see Trace's head. Unfortunately, she could see Logan clearly.

As he lifted two bales, one in each gloved hand, his biceps flexed and the muscles in his back moved as they tensed under the weight. His ass, covered in a pair of tight blue jeans with a bandana hanging out of his back pocket had her unable to look away until he strode out of sight. When he returned to the pile, he pulled off a glove, whipped the bandana out and wiped his face.

After putting the bandana away, he donned his glove again and lifted his arms to grasp two more bales. He'd just grabbed the hay, his muscles straining, when Trace spotted her and pointed.

Quickly, she tore her gaze from Logan and strode toward the forklift, the forks now resting on the floor of the barn. Cole noticed her and cut the engine, but she ignored him and stalked to Macy's stall. Relief and concern galloped through her.

She turned around in time to see Logan coming down the ladder. With more willpower than she knew she had, she turned toward Cole, who jumped down from the forklift. "Where is Macy and her baby?"

He opened his mouth to answer, but Logan stepped up. "They're outside."

She had no choice but to face him. "Outside?" It wasn't

hot yet, but it soon would be. "Where? Do they have shelter? Uncontaminated bedding? Was it really necessary to get a shipment of hay today?" Her voice rose with every question, her frayed nerves over Logan combined with her lack of sleep and her deep concern for the horses probably made her sound a little unreasonable.

"They're fine. Come, I'll show you." He turned toward the other two men. "I'll be right back."

She stared at the damp chest, dirtied with the hay and dust that covered his mounded pectorals. Her gaze flitted lower to his rippled abdominals where a trickle of sweat seeped below the waistline of his jeans. Instead of being repulsed, she felt a flutter of desire spread through her belly.

Logan turned back and opened his arm toward the barn entrance. "They're in the south corral."

She forced her gaze upward to meet his. Licking her lips, she finally stepped by him, wishing more than ever that she'd never met him in the first place. She was at the ranch more often than not, thanks to the rescue horses Cole brought in, so she was familiar with the south corral. The problem was, it had no shelter.

Stalking toward the area, her irritation at herself and Logan grew. As she stepped around the last outbuilding, she slowed. A new structure at the east side of the corral had been erected. Her anger dissipated and was replaced with a softening she could ill afford. She turned back to look at Logan. "You built them a shelter?"

He shrugged, not meeting her eyes. "There was already a roof because we had a youth group here a couple weeks ago. I just partially enclosed it."

Facing him hadn't been her smartest move, so she turned back and opened the corral gate. She needed to focus on the horses and go back to her office as soon as possible. She had appointments scheduled back-to-back this afternoon. She had to have her wits about her and not on a man that had made it perfectly clear he wasn't interested.

Then why the kiss last night?

As the horses came into view, she calmed. The foal was nodding its head and shuffling as if to play. Then it nudged its mom's teat and started suckling. "This boy knows what he wants and where he can get it." She smiled as she approached them.

"Most males do." Logan's voice behind her made her stiffen.

Was that what that kiss had been about? He wanted another night of meaningless sex? He was barking up the wrong tree for that. She didn't do meaningless sex...unfortunately, for her.

She lowered her bag to the ground and faced him again. "You can go back to hauling hay. I'm good here."

He raised his brows as if he doubted her abilities. "I'm glad I have your permission."

His sarcasm was clear, but she ignored it. Instead, she turned her back and opened her bag. "I work better alone, with no one getting in my way."

"Right."

She continued to shuffle through her bag before finding what she wanted. Then without looking behind her to see if Logan was still there, she approached mama. Macy watched her, so she stroked her on the neck first. The poor horse had terrible markings for a paint, making her face look more like a cow's. "What an amazing mom you are. You must be very proud." She kept her voice soft. She didn't want Macy getting too protective and literally kicking her out of the three-walled structure.

After making sure mama was doing well, she knelt on clean hay to inspect the foal, who broke off suckling to check her out. Her heart expanded as the horse nudged her shoulder. She chuckled quietly. "I'm not your mama, little one. Just here to make sure you grow up healthy and strong."

She performed a thorough examination but did so quickly, not wanting to test Macy's patience. Any mild-mannered mom could turn into a grizzly if she perceived her baby was threatened. When Jenna finished, she rose slowly and praised Macy again, finally checking to make sure Logan had left and happy to discover he had.

The foal went back to suckling and she left the two alone. As the first baby to be born on the horse rescue ranch, she couldn't help wonder what Cole would do with it. Luckily, that didn't need to be determined for a while.

She walked back to her bag and dropped her instruments into it. Hefting it over her shoulder, she exited the corral and headed to her car, giving the barn a wide berth. She had no idea when Logan had returned to work, but she was relieved he was there and not following her around.

As she approached her vehicle, she noticed a red convertible parked next to the hay truck. No one who lived at the ranch drove such an impractical car. Curious, she glanced toward the house. Had Lacey bought a new ride?

Unable to resist, she dropped her bag and strode to the house. The main door was open but the screen was closed, so she knocked on the frame. Annette's voice called for her to come in. She walked in to find Annette on the floor with Charlotte.

"Hi, I was just wondering if you had a bottle of water you could spare."

Annette nodded. "Of course, we do. Make yourself at home. You're here so often, I forget you don't live here. We tend to have a revolving door when it comes to residents."

Jenna chuckled. "Yes, you do, but I just work here."

"Too bad we couldn't make you a resident. I bet it would be cheaper than paying you to make house calls."

She tensed, but Annette waved her away. "I'm just kidding. Lacey has the finances under control. You're welcome here whether you're working or not." Annette returned her attention to Charlotte, who had crawled across the room and was in the process of climbing onto the empty second shelf of the entertainment center.

Jenna grinned as she made her way to the empty kitchen. Taking a water from the fridge, she unscrewed the cap and took a swallow. It didn't matter that the temperature was only in the nineties, the dry heat of Maricopa county required water all day every day.

Since the car outside was obviously not Lacey's, she walked back to the living room and leaned against the doorway. Annette had retrieved the toddler from the entertainment center and now sat about three feet from her. Charlotte was standing up, holding on to the outside of her playpen.

"Come on, sweetie. Come to Mimi. You can do it."

Charlotte squatted bending her knees like she would jump up in the air, but instead her small teddy bear flew at Annette.

The older woman caught it before it hit the floor, and Charlotte squealed.

"Great catch." Jenna toasted Annette with her bottle.

Annette looked over her shoulder at her. "I've had a lot of practice." She turned back to Charlotte. "Do you want your teddy bear?"

Charlotte reached out one hand and opened and closed her hand. "Mine. Mimi mine."

"Then come get it." Annette sat the teddy in her lap.

The concentration on Charlotte's face was captivating. She obviously wanted her bear, but wasn't sure what to do about it.

"Does she walk yet?"

Annette didn't look back, her entire concentration on the toddler. "Almost. She gets about one step then falls. I keep hoping."

Jenna held her breath as Charlotte let go of her playpen and took one step. She wobbled there for a moment then fell on her butt. She reached out her hand again. "Mine. Mimi."

"Then come and get it, sweetie."

Jenna released her breath. She would have loved to have seen Charlotte walk for the first time, but her family members deserved that privilege, especially Annette.

"No."

Annette leaned back on her hands. "Then how will you get it? I'm not bringing it to you."

Charlotte banged her hands on her thighs. "No. Mine." Now, her bottom lip stuck out and her little eyebrows furrowed.

Oh, Jenna knew those signs well. Her nephew was almost three, but he did the same thing at Charlotte's age. "I better get back to the office. Have fun, Annette."

Annette nodded, but didn't take her eyes off her great-grandchild. "Then come over here and get it."

She grinned as she left the standoff and headed outside. Charlotte wouldn't realize until she was older how lucky she was to have her great-grandmother. Jenna never knew her great-grandmother or her grandmother and her mother was only in her life for seven years, just long enough to make a wonderful impression and leave her with a constant heartache.

As she strode toward her car, she noticed the red convertible again. It was really none of her business, but she still found herself heading toward the barn.

She'd just let Cole know that Macy and the foal were doing well and she'd be back in a few months for vaccinations. She had no doubt she'd be called long before then because every rescue horse Cole brought to the ranch was given a thorough examination by her, and unfortunately, there were too many abused, neglected or unwanted horses discovered by animal welfare every week.

If she was lucky, she'd be able to talk to Cole without running in to Logan.

Chapter Three

From on top of the haybale stack, Logan heard the forklift engine cut off. Trace threw him another bale, and he placed it along the wall. The first truckload of hay he'd stacked when he first came to live on Last Chance had been with just Cole. Having Trace join the team had made them into a well-oiled machine, though he'd never admit that to his little brother.

At first, having Trace in his grandmother's house, sharing a room with old Billy, who snored, and spending an hour in the single upstairs bathroom had been far more than an irritation. It was too much like when they were boys with their petty rivalries and race to use the bathroom first. Charlotte refusing to sleep through the night didn't help his own mood either. But once his brother moved out, they got along fairly well.

If he could just get Trace to stop smiling all the damn time, he might actually like him. He turned to catch another bale, but Trace had disappeared. Now where did he go? Logan jumped down from the stack and walked to the edge of the hayloft.

Trace pointed up at him. "There he is. Hey, Logan, you have a visitor."

He moved his gaze to the woman in a short, flowered sundress that accented her tiny waist and long legs. Her blonde hair was straight and fine and some of it rested on one breast, though the breast itself wasn't very large. "Can I help you?"

She lifted her face to look at him and now her hand covered her chest. "You don't remember me?"

At her question, his gut tightened. Hell, those words could only mean one thing —a past one-night-stand had tracked him down. He hadn't even slept with a woman since moving to Last Chance and that was over a year and a half ago. If she'd found him, she was persistent. "Let me come down there."

He hooked his leg over the top rung and climbed down the ladder. She didn't look familiar, but with so many of the women he'd slept with having been picked-up in bars, the lighting was rarely that good and the sex tended toward a vehicle or motel room. The only ones he took back to his family's ranch were those from out of town.

When he reached the barn floor, he found Trace grinning at him and Cole frowning. Under his breath, he stepped up to Trace and muttered so only he could hear. "Give it a rest."

His affable brother just shook his head.

Logan turned toward the woman and doffed his cowboy hat. "I'm sorry, it's been a long time."

The woman with bright blue eyes beneath salon-styled eyebrows laughed. "Of course it has. Two years is a long time, but I'd hoped I hadn't changed that much since having the baby. I've worked really hard to get back into shape."

His face froze. Baby? "Ma'am, I'm afraid you have me at a disadvantage."

"Oh my. You really have no clue. Logan, I'm Kylie Bauer, your daughter's mother. I'm sorry about leaving her on your doorstep like that. I wasn't in a very good place in my life then, but I've changed. I have a steady job, own a car and I even took a lease on an apartment. I'm much more…"

Logan's heart froze. She wanted Charlotte! She couldn't have her! He tried to breathe, but his body wouldn't cooperate. When he finally sucked in air, he had to clamp his jaw shut to keep from yelling at the woman to get out. No one was taking Charlotte.

At a smack on his back, he looked behind him and scowled. "What?"

Trace gestured to the woman. "She asked you a question." Trace lowered his voice. "Come on, Logan, keep it together." It was the concern in Trace's eyes and the lack of smile that shocked him back into functioning.

He turned to Kylie, no memory of her surfacing, not even with her name. Had he really slept with that many women? Damn, he was an ass. "I'm sorry, ma'am. What did you ask?"

A flash of irritation crossed her face, but it was so quick he wasn't sure he saw it. "Our daughter. I asked if I could see her."

A deep-seated anger began to burn in his gut. It was the same feeling he had when he and his mother first found Charlotte on his doorstep. Despite denying she was his, he'd been enraged that a woman, a mother, could do such a thing.

He scowled. "*Now* you want to see her? I think you gave up that right fourteen months ago when you abandoned her."

Kylie frowned and clasped her hands. "I wouldn't have been good for her. I knew she would be safe with you." She looked away. "I was in a bad place then, but I'm better now." She faced him again. "Please."

"What do you mean 'a bad place?'" It had been too many months without hearing from her, without any explanation as to why she left his daughter on his family's porch down near Catalina, and now he was determined to get it.

Again, she wouldn't meet his eyes. "I'd been doing things that weren't exactly lawful to make some money." Her gaze flew back to him. "Nothing like selling my body or anything, just... just worked for the wrong people."

And what if she still works for those people? The prospect was chilling. "No, you can't see Charlotte."

She snapped her head around and her eyes widened. "Is that what you named her? Charlotte?" She said the word as if getting used to it. "I like it. Very old fashioned."

He didn't give a damn if she liked it or not. He wanted her to leave and for good. He put his hat back on. "If you'll excuse me, I have to get back to work."

"Wait!" Kylie took a step toward him. "Can't we talk about this? I mean, after all, I am...Charlotte's mother. I should be allowed to see her."

"Logan." Trace had stepped closer to whisper. "You should at least listen to what she has to say, for Charlotte's sake."

Hell. He took off his gloves and cracked the knuckles on one hand. He should do what was right for his daughter, but every fatherly instinct he had made him want to yell "mine" at the top of his lungs like his daughter did.

He stared long and hard at Kylie. Nothing about her triggered even the slightest memory. He couldn't believe he had been so lost in sex as to not recognize a woman after only a couple years. It was probably one of his backseat episodes. Then and there he vowed to never tell Charlotte where she'd been conceived.

"Please, Logan. I want to explain everything." She looked at him with puppy dog eyes.

Damn. "I can meet you at the Black Mustang bar tomorrow night at eight."

"Will you bring Charlotte?"

"What? No." He scowled again. What woman brought her toddler to a bar?

She quickly back-pedaled. "I'm sorry. I just got excited."

"I'll meet you there to talk. That's it." The last thing he wanted to do was sleep with her again. He loved his daughter and he was glad she was conceived, but Kylie did nothing for him. Maybe his tastes had changed.

"Got it. The Black Mustang at eight. I'll be there. Thank you." She nodded then turned. "Oh, hi."

Logan's gut tensed as Kylie sashayed out only to reveal Jenna standing at the entrance to the barn. How long had she been there?

She nodded once to Kylie then strode past him and addressed Cole. "Macy and the baby are in good health. They won't need any vaccinations for a few months."

That she ignored him, pissed him off. He was the one who took care of the horses after the birth. He was the one who would own the foal. Before Cole could respond, he stepped between them. "Good. I'll call you if they need anything else."

She lowered her brow. "I would think you have other matters to attend to that are more important than the horses."

So, she did hear everything. Damn.

She stepped around him to talk to Cole again. "I believe Lightyear and Black Jack are due for vaccinations then too, but I'll check my records when I get back to the office. It will cost you less if I can do them all on the same day."

Cole looked at him as if inviting him to answer, but he kept his mouth shut. Finally, his cousin replied to her. "That sounds good, but we'll need you back here later this week if you can fit us in. I have a new horse arriving from Texas."

"The horse you told me about? The one burned in the barn fire?"

"Yes. The vet in Dallas took great care of him, but I'm pretty sure this will be his forever home. I'd like you to check him out."

"I'd be happy to. Do you mind if Whisper does as well?"

Cole chuckled. "I don't think it's a matter of what I want when it comes to Whisper."

She gave Cole a fleeting smile. "True. Call my office as far in advance as you can. If I can schedule around the horse's arrival time, I will, but if not, I'll just come out after office hours."

"Thank you." Cole put his hand on Jenna's arm.

Logan barely suppressed a growl. What the hell? Cole wasn't just his cousin but married to boot. He was being unreasonable, as his mom used to say.

Jenna shrugged, dislodging Cole's hand. "It's what I do and as Last Chance is my biggest and best client, I'm more than happy to oblige." She gave Cole a nod and turned to leave.

"I'll walk you out." Now why the hell did he say that?

She didn't look at him. "Don't bother. I know my way."

He knew that. He also knew that both his brother and his cousin were looking at him like he'd lost his senses, but he still found his legs carrying him alongside Jenna.

Once outside and around the corner of the barn, she stopped. "What are you doing?"

Her words were clearly ground out between clenched teeth.

It gave him a perverse pleasure to know someone else was as irritated as he was. He smirked. "I'm walking you to your car."

She faced him and crossed her arms over her chest. "Since when?"

Good question. "Since I wanted to ask you to go to the Black Mustang tomorrow night."

Her eyes widened in shock before she dropped her arms and hooked a thumb over her shoulder. "I thought you were meeting Charlotte's mother there tomorrow night."

Now that he'd said it, a plan started to form. "I am. That's why I want you there. You're a no nonsense kind of person. I need someone else's opinion of her."

He pushed his left hand against his thigh, cracking three knuckles at once before continuing. "My family will tell me to let her see Charlotte simply because she's her mother, but I need to know she's acceptable. I don't want to expose Charlotte to her mother if she's a druggy, or shady or anything else that could be dangerous."

Jenna looked at him oddly. "Logan Williams, I don't know whether to kick your ass or hug you."

At the thought of her throwing her tiny body against his, his mind skittered in another direction all together. Damn, he still had it bad for her. This probably wasn't such a good idea. "Never mind. It was just an idea."

"I'll go."

"What?" Now he was certain he was hearing things.

Jenna shrugged. "It's not like I have anything else to do tomorrow night, and I'll admit to a certain curiosity about Charlotte's mother. So sure, I'll go." She squinted her eyes at him. "But you owe me one."

Excitement and nerves tangled in his gut. His inner child was jumping up and down while his more sensible self tried to warn him he was screwed. "Right."

Jenna opened her rear car door and threw her heavy bag onto the seat. If his grandmother had seen how he walked Jenna to her car without taking her bag, he'd get an earful. Why couldn't he act normal around the woman?

She opened the driver side door and glanced at him. "See you tomorrow night." Then she ducked inside and started the engine.

He stood where he was, watching her back out, turn around, and head down the dirt driveway. He was an idiot or a genius, he wasn't sure which. Either way, tomorrow night would prove to be interesting. After all, what could possibly go wrong having two women he'd slept with meet him at a bar.

Definitely an idiot.

Jenna stopped looking at her reflection in her rearview mirror. This was stupid. She was here to gauge the character of Charlotte's mother. She wasn't here on a date with the only man to break her heart.

Then why had she worn make-up and an actual skirt? To be fair, it was a jean skirt and fell halfway down her brown cowboy boots. Her usual white button-down collared shirt was long sleeved since the desert could be cool at night in September, and her blue suede vest matched her skirt perfectly.

It was a far cry from the spaghetti-strap top, short shorts and boots she'd worn the afternoon she'd met Logan. She'd been open to a relationship then, still was, only not with the man whose truck was parked on the other side of the dirt parking lot of the Black Mustang.

Maybe she'd get lucky and another man inside would find her interesting. She'd love to show Logan Williams that he'd thrown away a real prize.

She put her cowboy hat on and tucked in a few loose strands. She was such a Pollyanna to think that suddenly, after years of lackluster success, she'd finally find the man of her dreams in a bar just down the road from her dilapidated old log home.

"Hope springs eternal." Pulling the keys from the ignition, she palmed them and got out of her little sedan. Scanning the parking lot again, she didn't spot the red convertible. She checked her watch and frowned. She'd hoped not to be alone with Logan.

After locking her car, she strode toward the wooden porch. In front was an old-fashioned horse trough, though the place was only a couple decades old. Whoever owned the place had her dad's penchant for replicating the Old West. Above the porch hung a wooden sign with a black mustang galloping toward the letters declaring it the Black Mustang Saloon.

She walked up the four steps and pulled open the door. Inside the lights were low except for in the far corner where a few bikers were playing pool. She scanned the tables but didn't see Logan. A country song started to blare from the juke box and she looked there, but it was a young woman who had started it.

She walked toward the bar. There were a few construction workers hanging out at one end, a husband and wife in the middle and a few cowboys taking up the three seats on the near end. Her gaze stopped on the one closest to her. Fudge, she'd know that back anywhere. Luckily, he'd covered it up with a red plaid shirt, but it didn't stop her from remembering what it looked like earlier in the day.

What was she doing? She should leave. But even as she started to turn away, one of the other cowboys noticed her.

"Whoa Nellie, what do we have here?" He rose and doffed his hat. "Miss, if you need a seat at the bar, you can have mine."

The other cowboy turned as well to see who his friend spoke to, but Logan remained as he was. What happened to the charmer from the county fair? "No, thank you. I'm meeting someone."

The cowboy's shoulders fell. "All the good ones are taken."

He resumed his seat so he missed her shaking her head. She needed to get out more often.

Unfortunately, she was out now and Logan had turned around at the sound of her voice. "You came." He sounded surprised.

Yeah, probably not the smartest move she ever made. Best to keep to the task at hand. "Where is she?"

He waved down the bartender then shrugged. "She hasn't come yet." He turned his head to face the bartender. "Cutter, I'll take two more beers."

She stepped up to the bar. "If one of those is for me, make it a ginger ale."

Logan raised an eyebrow but just nodded to the bartender. When their drinks came, Logan opened his arm toward the room of tables.

She found one near the door she'd come in. If she needed to make a hasty exit, she'd prefer to have the shortest route possible. Logan pulled out a chair for her and she sat. Then he took the chair next to her and swung it around to straddle it. Great, his legs were spread wide, his knee almost touching her leg.

"Did you get here on time? Maybe she came already and you weren't here."

He shook his head. "Not a chance. I've been here since six."

"Six?" She took another good look at him. Had he been drinking all that time?

"Don't look at me like that. This is only my third beer."

Busted, she focused on her drink and had a sip. She put the glass down. "So, what do you want me to do?"

Logan sighed. "I don't know, for sure. I guess I want an impartial, second opinion."

"You do know, if she really is Charlotte's mom, you can't legally keep her from her daughter." Nor should he want to. Whatever Charlotte's mother had done, if she was back, Charlotte deserved to know her. Jenna would be thrilled if her mom came back.

"If? What are you saying?" He frowned, but that was pretty common for him.

"If you really want to protect your daughter, you should require a DNA test. I'm sure she is her mother because who else would come looking for you except Charlotte's mom?" Fudge, was it her or did she sound resentful? Hopefully, Logan was too worried about his daughter to notice.

"You're right. I'll do that first. But if she is as she claims, I can't let her take Charlotte."

She must not have any self-preservation genes at all because the worry in Logan's voice had her melting. She touched his arm. "My dad always says not to borrow trouble. It'll find you soon enough, so don't assume the worst. Find out what her life is like now. She may just want to have visitation rights."

Logan took a gulp of beer, his Adam's apple moving the fine stubble along his neck. The remembered scrape of that stubble along her inner thigh had her crossing her legs. How was she supposed to remain impartial when she was half in love with him and pissed off at him at the same time?

"Here she is." Logan's low voice sent another memory of them in bed skittering through her head, and she forcefully pushed it away to study the woman she'd seen in the barn.

Kylie was dressed in a white, short-sleeved blouse with a scooped neckline giving her a delicate, helpless look. Her pink-flowered, very short skirt hugged her abdomen then flared out in a ruffle about four inches wide. She wore strappy pink heels that crisscrossed up to her ankles, her perfectly straight blonde hair was pulled away from her heart-shaped face with a pink headband and to complete the ensemble, she carried a tiny pink pocketbook over her shoulder. The word "clueless" came to mind, but Jenna refused to stereotype. After all, this was Charlotte's mom.

She tried to picture the woman in front of her holding Charlotte and couldn't. Maybe she was biased because she had to be at least five years older than Kylie.

Kylie scanned the bar and when her gaze lit on Logan she smiled. She started forward. It took her a moment before she realized Jenna sat there as well. Kylie came to a stop before smiling at her too. Now, that was telling. Jenna would bet a dollar to donuts Kylie was looking for one big happy family with Logan.

At that observation, the ginger ale in her stomach started to eat away at her insides.

"Hi, Logan. Thank you for meeting so we can talk." Kylie took the seat across from them and looked at Jenna. "I'm sorry, I don't know you. My name is Kylie."

"I'm Dr. Jenna Atkins." She left it at that.

Kylie's eyebrows rose. "You're a doctor?"

"A veterinary doctor."

"Oh, that's why you were at the ranch." Kylie returned her focus to Logan, dismissing Jenna as unimportant.

She bristled, but the fact was, she *was* unimportant in Logan's life. She was only helping him out with this. No, she wasn't helping him. She was here for Charlotte. Charlotte loved her daddy, not knowing what a jerk he could be. And Annette's whole day was centered on the little girl. Everyone on the Last Chance doted on Charlotte. If she was taken from there...

"Please, Logan, I just want to see my little girl. I'll tell you anything you want to know." Kylie leaned forward in entreaty.

Logan, in turn, leaned back. "Why now? It's been fourteen months since you left my month-old daughter on my parents' porch in the middle of the winter. It was almost freezing at Ragged Peaks ranch that night. What kind of mother could do that? Or *was* it you? Did you have someone do your dirty work for you?"

"No, no. I did it, but she was in no danger. I knocked and waited to make sure someone found her."

Logan's gaze turned cold. "If you were there, who found her?"

She blinked. "Who? It was a woman. I'm guessing your mother?"

Jenna could feel Logan's tension as his leg pushed against her own. She should move away, but she felt she was helping him keep his cool in some way, and he definitely needed to do that.

"My mother and I called out. Why didn't you come? If you were there, you could have at least explained why you were getting rid of your own daughter."

Kylie leaned back and put her hands in her lap. "I wasn't 'getting rid' of her. I was turning her care over to you because I couldn't be sure of her safety with me."

"Why?" Logan's tone was hard as nails.

She looked away. "I was working for a fence in Phoenix and not everything was working out very well. A sheriff was on to him and the men we were getting goods from were not the nicest."

"If you were working with criminals, then what were you doing in Catalina? That's at least seventy miles from south Phoenix."

This time she looked down at her hands as if she were ashamed. "I had been visiting my sister to hide out for a while. My boss would have thrown me under the bus if he got caught."

"Did he?"

She shook her head. "No. He was smarter than that. He moved his operation to Tucson." She finally raised her head. "I told him I couldn't go because of my family."

"When did this happen?" Logan frowned with his direct concentration.

Kylie looked startled by the question. "Around Thanksgiving."

"It's September. I ask you again. Why now?"

"I told you at the ranch, because I needed to get a job and a new place to live."

"Because you were living with your boss."

Kylie scanned the bar, ignoring Logan's statement. "Is there a cocktail waitress here?"

When it was obvious Logan wasn't going to answer, Jenna addressed Kylie. "No, you have to go to the bar to buy a drink."

Kylie rose. "Wow, I guess this really is the boonies." She immediately turned and walked to the bar.

"I don't remember her." Logan's voice sounded anguished.

She had no sympathy for him there. "You probably don't remember all of them. From what Trace told me, you had quite a few 'flings' as he put it."

Logan turned and faced her. "I remember you." His face had softened.

Darn it. Just as she worked up a good, healthy anger, he undercut it. "Yeah, well, I'm kind of memorable when you run into me at your cousin's three months later."

He continued to stare at her, his expression unreadable. Finally, he turned back and took a gulp of beer. "I thought Charlotte's mother would be more…"

When he didn't continue, she tried to supply a word for him. "Upright? Pretty? Sweet?"

He shook his head. "Quality."

In that, they were in agreement. There was nothing about Kylie's appearance that had her thinking she was a slut or an assistant fence or anything like that. It was more an aura about her, not that Jenna believed in auras. That was a Sedona thing. It was more a sense she had about the woman.

Kylie returned to the table and sat down with a shot and a beer. "I hope you don't mind, but this conversation calls for a little whiskey." She threw down the shot and took a sip of beer.

Logan pounced on that. "Why is this conversation so hard?"

She scowled. "Because I don't tell my life story to just anyone. I'm not proud of what I've done. Like I said. I'm back on track now."

Logan set his arms across the back of the chair in front of him. "Tell me about our night together."

Chapter Four

Jenna cringed. The last thing she wanted to hear about was Logan having sex with another woman.

Kylie glanced at her. "Are you sure?"

"I can leave for a moment." She started to push back her chair.

Logan's hand shot out and grasped her thigh. "No. I want you to stay."

What was he doing? He knew this was awkward.

"Go ahead. Tell me." Logan's gaze was on Kylie, but his hand continued to grasp her leg, heating her from the inside out.

"Okay. Well, we met at Jed's bar. We flirted and danced and within a couple hours we left together." She picked up her beer and drank.

"Then what?" Logan's concentration was intense.

She lowered her beer. "Then we ended up in the back of your truck. There were no lights out there, so it was relatively private."

"Did we take our clothes off?"

Jenna swallowed a groan. Wasn't this special? When he'd brought her back to his family's ranch, he'd made a production of kissing away every inch of clothing, including her panties. The memory alone made her palms sweat.

"Only what was needed. You were in a hurry, so we just pushed things aside." Kylie quickly took another gulp of beer.

Logan squeezed her thigh hard, but his body language was completely relaxed. He even quirked the corner of his lips. "So, if I let you see Charlotte, will you be happy with that? Will you leave her alone for me to raise like you originally intended?"

She clasped her hands together and looked down at them. "I don't know. I just want to see my baby."

Jenna relaxed as Logan finally let go of her thigh. Him touching her made it hard to concentrate on the issue at hand.

He took a swig of his own beer, only the second since she'd come in. "I will let you see Charlotte on two conditions."

Kylie's face lit with anticipation. "Name it. Anything you want. Even if you want me."

He shook his head, much to Jenna's relief. She didn't know what Kylie was up to, but she was darn sure that Logan sleeping with her would only make it worse for him. Or was that her own jealousy coming into play?

"First, I want a DNA test from you to prove you're Charlotte's mom."

"What? Of course, I am. Who else could it be? That could take a week. Please tell me you won't make me wait that long."

"Second, I want in writing what your intentions are regarding Charlotte."

"But I just told you I don't know. I won't know until I see my baby girl."

Jenna almost felt sorry for the woman, but not quite. Kylie gave off a vibe that said please take care of me, something Jenna had never been able to pull off. She'd started working at age fifteen to help her dad with their expenses. Her younger sister had started at that age too, and it was the only way they'd been able to keep the homestead.

47

"Those are my terms." Logan lifted his beer in salute. "Take them or leave them." He brought the beer to his mouth, but he barely drank. What was he up to?

Kylie worried her bottom lip, but didn't say anything. As the silence dragged out, Jenna uncrossed her legs and rose. "If you two don't mind, I need to use the ladies room. I'll be back."

"I'll come with you." Kylie rose quickly. "It was a long drive from Phoenix."

Jenna nodded and strode between the tables to the restroom, Kylie's heels making far more noise than her own boots. Once inside, she made a beeline for the closest stall.

When she came out, she found Kylie waiting for her. So much for having to use the facilities.

"Doc, do you think Logan will budge on this? I'm guessing you're a good friend if he brought you. You must understand what it's like for a mother to want to hold her own child. Is there anything you could do to sway him?"

She moved to the sink to wash her hands, not sure which question to answer or if she wanted to answer any of them. She was far too sympathetic to the mother-daughter relationship. Since the night her own father made her mother leave, she'd always wanted to find her, but she couldn't do that to him. "I have no influence over Logan. In fact, if I suggested one thing, he'd just do the opposite. That's his modus operandi around me."

Kylie turned to the mirror and reapplied her lipstick. The light pink color matched everything else on her. "I don't need you to operate. I just need you to help me convince him."

Grabbing a few paper towels, she faced the woman. "That's what I'm trying to tell you. He won't listen to me."

Kylie squinted her eyes. "You just don't want to help me. Then I'll find another way to influence him." She pulled her top down lower as if to show her cleavage, but she really didn't have any to boast of. Then she sashayed out of the restroom.

Jenna leaned against the wall as she dried her hands. She sincerely hoped Charlotte had inherited her father's brains because her mother didn't appear to be that smart. Then again, it could simply be a lack of education. Kylie could be very smart, but like Jenna's own sister, didn't have any schooling after high school.

Walking to the trash can, she dropped her paper towel in it and opened the door. Hopefully, she'd given them enough time to come to terms and she could go home. When she turned the corner into the main area of the bar, her gaze found Logan right away, but he sat at the table alone.

She pulled out her chair and joined him. Logan appeared deep in thought, so she finished off her ginger ale and waited. She couldn't imagine what it must be like for him. When he'd first come to Cole's Last Chance horse rescue ranch, he seemed to resent his fatherhood, but that could have been because Charlotte never slept through the night. Back then, even relaxed Trace was grumpy.

It hadn't been hard to notice a change. As a person who visited the ranch almost once a week, she'd observed the growing connection between him and his daughter. He still had some underlying anger or resentment going on inside, but it didn't seem directed at Charlotte. If anything, his connection to Charlotte had softened some of his sharp edges.

When she first met him, he was all charm and smiles, but there was an edge about him that she'd been nervous about. In their one day together, she hadn't figured out what it was, but in light of his interest in her and their mutual attraction, she'd forgotten her worries. That wasn't the only thing she'd forgotten. She'd completely ignored her strict rules against going beyond a kiss on a first date.

Staring at his profile, her stomach did a little flip. That day at the Pima Harvest fair, he'd swept her off her feet. Naively, she'd thought it was fate. Turned out to be a fatality for her heart. The next morning when he'd dropped her off at her car, he had given no indication she would never see him again. In fact, he didn't seem to want to let her go, even giving her his phone number, but despite her numerous messages over a couple weeks, he never called her back. Was that what he did with all his one day conquests?

She frowned as her hurt resurfaced. After she returned home to Wickenburg, she'd been at Last Chance vaccinating a new arrival when Cole mentioned his lover-boy cousin Logan would be moving in. She never put two and two together since they had different last names. Though what good it would have done her was beyond her. She'd still be the vet for Last Chance and the man sitting beside her would still be living there. So, what was she doing at a bar with him?

Charlotte. She needed to keep her emotions in check and focus on Charlotte. Not because the toddler was Logan's, but because she was a sweet new human being who deserved to be protected and loved. No matter what Jenna thought about Logan, he did that for his daughter. Maybe she was just jealous he didn't do the same for her.

He finally turned and looked at her. His gaze was thoughtful as he seemed to take inventory of her face.

"What? Do I have something on my cheek?" She brushed at her face.

His lip quirked up a bit. "No. I was just thinking about the day I discovered Charlotte was really mine."

"You mean when she was left on your doorstep?" She couldn't believe Kylie had done that.

He shook his head, his lip quirking up a bit more. "The day

I got the DNA results. Kylie is right. In Phoenix, it may take a few days but out in Catalina, the test had to be sent out and it was a good two weeks. The first day of having Charlotte in the house, she had no name and I refused to give her one. I was absolutely certain she wasn't mine because I was always very careful."

He looked away. At least he had the grace to feel uncomfortable around her. Not only had she been on the pill, but he'd insisted on condoms. She'd thought he was being protective, but he obviously had personal motives as well. Still, she wanted to hear the rest of the story. "So, what happened?"

Logan grinned. The type of grin that had completely swept her off her feet. "I fell hard for my girl. Charlotte took my heart within the first twenty-four hours and wouldn't let go, and I mean that almost literally. The minute I handed her to my mother, she would lose her smile and whimper. She made it so hard to work the ranch."

He shook his head. "When just before dinner that fateful night, my mother gave me the envelope that came in the mail, I had to leave the kitchen. The first night I saw Charlotte, I was so sure she wasn't mine, but as I held that envelope, I contemplated throwing it in the fire pit to be burned up at the next gathering."

"But you didn't." She could imagine the whole scene, especially since she had tiptoed through that very kitchen on her way out before dawn broke. She could see him leaving the room, his semi-long hair back then caught back in a small ponytail, his hands dirty from branding cattle or digging up a rotten fence pole, his strong fingers clutching the un-opened envelope.

"No, I didn't. I *had* to know, but in that moment, I knew I would keep her. I just needed to know if I would have to fight for her. When I saw we were definitely related, I yelled."

He shrugged. "I guess I didn't do that very much because my mother ran in with Charlotte in her arms to find out what was wrong. I took my daughter from her and shared the news that she was a grandmother."

He chuckled. "You should have seen the look on her face. I don't think she had fully realized she was old enough to be a grandmother. She stood still, her mouth open, for a good minute and a half."

Jenna smiled, the story warming her heart.

But Logan lost his. "I never expected Charlotte's mother to show up. As far as I was concerned, she'd lost her chance to be a mother. What kind of mother could leave her baby on a doorstep in the middle of the night?"

She didn't know what to say. Having met Kylie, she had a feeling she'd actually done the right thing. She also thought coming back to try to have a relationship with her daughter was the right thing, but she kept that to herself. It would be a lot easier if Kylie had been a little more trustworthy. Jenna could understand Logan's concern. She had a feeling it was the same reason her dad threw her own mother out, but he refused to talk about that.

Logan cracked the knuckles on his right hand as if he didn't realize he did it. She didn't remember him having that habit the day she met him. "I didn't expect Kylie to be Charlotte's mom. I always kind of pictured you."

She widened her eyes. "Me?" She almost choked. "Why me? You think I could be so callous? You think a woman who will go to any length to save four premature kittens would drop my child off like that?" The hurt in her chest was making it difficult to speak.

"No, no. Never." Logan grabbed her hand. "That's not what I meant. Or not what I thought. No, I mean, I had hoped

Charlotte had inherited some of her intelligence, looks and character from someone like you. Someone with integrity."

She couldn't wrap her brain around his upside-down compliment though her heart warmed. Instead, she pulled her hand from his. "I think I know what you mean, not that it matters." She set her empty glass toward the center of the table and pushed her chair back. "I'm guessing Kylie left, so I better get home. I have an early vaccination appointment tomorrow—a couple of new calves."

She stood to keep herself from rambling any more.

"I'll walk you out." As Logan rose, she headed for the door. He still managed to open it for her.

Once on the porch, he put a hand on her shoulder. "Whoa, slow down. You haven't told me what you think of Kylie? Do you think I should let her see Charlotte?"

She stopped because to keep walking would be too rude. "She seems honest though I don't like her background. But you need to think about what happens if you don't let her see her daughter. If you get her too mad, she may go to a judge and force the issue. Once she does that, you'll have the justice system involved."

"I don't want that. Charlotte belongs with me."

The more they talked about Charlotte, the easier it was for her to ignore her own feelings. "Did she agree to your terms before she left?"

"No. She said she needed to think about it and would call me."

That could mean she wanted Charlotte but was afraid to tell Logan. Or... "She could want you three to be one big happy family."

Logan shuddered. "First, she wouldn't be a good influence on Charlotte. Second, I'm not the least attracted to her, so if that is her intention, we may need to go to court after all."

Jenna frowned. "Wait, you got her pregnant even though you weren't attracted to her? How does that work?"

"I don't know. Maybe it was dark?"

"Really, Logan? It had to be pretty darn dark. Here we are in an unlit parking lot with only a bar sign and a couple neon signs in the windows for light, and I can tell what you look like."

"I know." He curled his hand into a fist.

"Were you drunk?" She could see that happening. One of her friends in college ended up pregnant that way.

He shook his head. "I've never buried my sorrows in a bottle."

Her curiosity took notice. "Then how do you bury your sorrows?"

His gaze became intense. "With sex." He took a step closer. "I find an attractive, hot, willing woman and make love to her, burying my sorrow deep while I find bliss in our joint climax."

She knew he'd been blunt on purpose, but the way he looked at her when he said the words made tingles skitter across her skin and an ache start in her belly. She swallowed hard and ignored her body. "Well, Kylie is definitely interested. She said as much in the restroom."

That cooled him down a bit. "What else did she say?"

"She wanted me to encourage you to let her see Charlotte. I told her that wouldn't work because everything I tell you, you do the opposite."

His head jerked back a fraction. "I do?"

She sighed. "Yes, you do. I don't know why you have to argue with me about everything. I'm a certified, degree-carrying veterinarian."

Logan's look turned sheepish. "I can't help it."

"Yes, you can. All you have to do is say, 'Good idea Dr.

Jenna'." Now that they were discussing it, she was glad to get it out in the open.

He shook his head. "I can't."

She crossed her arms over her chest. "And why can't you?"

The intensity returned to his gaze. "Because if I don't fight with you, I'll end up kissing you."

Stunned, she stared at him while her heart galloped hard in her chest.

His big hands cupped her face. "Jenna." His voice, so low and husky, pulled her in. "When I'm with you, I want to touch you, so I fight it and you, but I don't want to fight it anymore."

As her heart leapt at his words, her entire body came alive with the touch of his lips on hers. She moved her hands to his hard chest as his tongue swept into her mouth, tasting her like she was a craving he couldn't deny.

One of his hands cupped her head and his other moved down her back to pull her closer. She felt the bulge of his rising need which set her nipples on fire. She slid her arms up and around his neck as his tongue tangled with her own.

He tasted of beer and man and everything that made her want him. His hard chest pressed against her breasts and her body ignited with remembered passion. He backed off the kiss by nibbling on her lips and kissing the corner of her mouth.

She didn't want him to stop, but the bray of a wild burrow in the distance recalled her to where she was, in a dirt parking lot outside a bar. She pulled her head back to look at him. "Why did you do that?" She hadn't meant to say the words aloud, but since they were out, she was anxious for his reply.

His broad shoulders shrugged. "Instinct."

"Instinct?" She pulled her arms down and pushed against his chest. "Instinct is what guides animals, not us. We have brains." Darn, she was no more than a mating call to him. "We have hearts." He finally let her step away, the catch in her voice telling more than she wanted it to.

"Wait. Maybe that was the wrong word."

Sure, and maybe it was exactly the right one. He was drawn to her for sex because she was in the corral. Best to get this filly far away from Mr. Stud. "Goodnight, Logan." She spun on her heel and stomped to her car.

"Jenna, wait!"

She couldn't wait. He'd tear her heart apart again. Hearing his cowboy boots crunching across the dirt parking lot behind her, she quickly unlocked the car door and reached for the handle, but Logan's hand surrounded hers.

"Jenna, listen to me." He pulled on her hand, forcing her to face him. "I used the wrong word. I should have said self-preservation is what motivated me to kiss you."

She opened her mouth to tell him that was no different, but he squeezed her hand and shook his head.

"You don't understand. I had to kiss you because I can't stop thinking of us, like we were when we liked each other, instead of whatever this is." Though he held her hand, he gestured between them with his other.

The last place she wanted to return to was their time together. Didn't he get it? She was trying to forget it. "So, what are you saying? That you want to sleep with me again for 'old times' sake?"

He let go of her hand. "Not for old times' sake. Maybe for new time's sake?" He attempted a pitiful smirk.

Why didn't her heart understand what an ass he could be? "I'll tell you what you told Kylie. First, get tested and prove to me you don't carry any sexual diseases and second, write down what you want from me."

He scowled. "Don't throw my own words back at me."

She crossed her arms. "Then don't throw my mistake back at me."

"What mistake?"

She threw up her hands. "If you can't figure that out then I can't help you." She spun around and yanked her door open. Slamming it shut, she started the car and drove by him, her heart pounding and her stomach tied up in a knot that was so tight, she thought she would vomit.

She pulled onto the highway and hit the gas. He just didn't understand what torture he was for her. Maybe she *did* need to give up Last Chance. If she had one more conversation with him, she was sure she'd either break down in tears or hit him over the head with a shovel.

Chapter Five

Logan closed the tabs on Charlotte's diaper. The teddy bear with the cowboy hat was firmly in her mouth and her cheeks were flushed. She wasn't talking much this morning, just humming. It must be another tooth coming in. Her first teeth took forever, but as more popped up, she seemed to weather them better.

Pretty soon she'd be brushing her own teeth. He'd just found her fourteen months ago but she'd grown, according to the doctor, right on schedule. But it was too fast. He picked up his bundle of sweetness and moved to the dresser to take out a pair of purple overalls and a pink t-shirt.

Closing the drawer, he laid her on the bed and pulled the shirt over her head, dislodging the teddy. She immediately made a grab for it and almost fell off the bed, but he caught her, his heart pounding at the near fall. His grandmother said Charlotte wasn't a China doll and would fall a hundred times a week and survive, but not on his watch.

He set her back on the bed and picked up the teddy.

"Mine." She held out her hand.

"Can you say please?"

"Mine." She frowned. "Mine, da-da!"

He shook his head. "Say please."

Charlotte popped her mouth open and closed it, her face scrunching before she gave a sharp and short screech.

"Ouch, that hurt." Cole, dressed in his fire department blue t-shirt, stepped into the room, his hands over his ears.

Logan held the teddy in front of his daughter. "Please, da-da."

Her little face started to pucker, her bottom lip pushing out and he caved. Handing her the teddy, which she promptly put in her mouth, he kissed her on the forehead. "You *will* learn your manners."

Cole chuckled. "What she's learning is how to wrap her daddy around her little finger."

Logan pulled the overalls up and buttoned them over her shoulders. "Too late. That's already happened."

As if she knew she was mostly dressed, she rolled over on to her tummy and pushed herself backwards until her feet touched the floor. With the teddy in her mouth and one hand holding onto the quilt, she walked to the end of the bed to look at Cole.

"Are you coming to your Uncle Cole for a hug?" Cole crouched down.

Logan pulled out a pair of socks. "Technically, you're her second cousin."

Cole ignored him. "Come on, sweetie."

Charlotte took one step toward him before falling back on her butt.

Logan watched his daughter crawl to Cole. "I think something's wrong with her balance. I asked my mom and she said both Trace and I were walking by now."

Cole scooped up Charlotte, who giggled as he blew her kisses. "I wouldn't worry about it. My mom always complained that Dillon and I had spoiled her by waiting to the last minute to walk then she ended up exhausted from chasing after us. She said we were making up for lost time."

Logan put socks on his daughter's feet while Cole held her. "That's reassuring...I think."

Cole laughed and handed Charlotte over. "It's all how you look at it. Listen, I have a horse coming in today. I was actually supposed go to Dallas to pick it up, but I couldn't get off work, so my friend Bo and his girlfriend Dana have been driving since yesterday, but when they arrive, Lacey and I won't be here. Can you get the horse settled in and turn them over to Gram?"

Logan put Charlotte in the crook of his arm. "Of course. Did you already tell Gram?"

"Yes. Lacey had me bring over a tray of hors d'oeuvres for them. Don't eat any."

Logan stepped by his cousin. "As if I would."

Cole followed him downstairs. "That's right, you prefer breakfast food. I also called Jenna to let her know. She's going to come by after she closes, but I won't get off shift until Thursday. She said she wanted to talk to me about something. Do you have any idea what it could be?"

He shrugged in response even as he swallowed hard and his gut tensed.

"You haven't done anything worse than usual, have you?"

His cousin's assumption hit too close to home. When he reached the bottom of the stairs, he stopped. "Why do you think it's about me?"

Cole faced him as he came to a stop at the bottom of the landing. "I don't know. I just have this feeling in my gut that she may not want to be our vet anymore and that would really throw a wrench in the works, just when I have this place finally running smoothly. The next closest vet is all the way in New

River. Besides, Jenna is a damn good vet." He glared. "You better remember that."

Charlotte pulled the teddy out of her mouth and thrust it at Cole. "Kissie bye-bye."

Cole switched his attention and Logan took a steadying breath. Was his cousin, right? Would Jenna stop coming to Last Chance? He didn't want that at all. He may not know what he wanted with Jenna, but not seeing her was definitely not his answer. It was bad enough he hadn't seen her in two days, which was stupid. He'd gone longer than that before, but that was before he started kissing her again.

After Cole kissed the teddy and Charlotte, he patted him on the shoulder. "And don't worry. Bo and Dana are coming to my house as soon as Lacey gets home. You'll still have the house to yourself with Gram and Gramps, when Gramps is home that is."

So that was his silver lining on the day. There may be one bedroom technically free in the house, but there was only one upstairs bathroom and it would still be his.

As the front door closed behind his cousin, he headed for the kitchen where Gram would be waiting to feed her great-granddaughter. He was pleased his daughter had one constant female presence in her life. Would Kylie confuse Charlotte?

Kylie showing up out of the blue was just another piece of bad luck piled onto the rest. He'd never believed in universal fate or any of that bull crap, but ever since his father had his first stroke, fate had decided to deal him one losing hand after another.

"There's my girl." Gram reached for Charlotte as he walked in, and he handed her over.

"She's getting heavy, Gram. Be careful."

His grandmother scowled at him. "I'm no frail old lady, Logan. Seventy-two does not mean I have one foot in the grave."

He cringed. "I would never think that."

While she settled Charlotte into the high chair, he grabbed three of her homemade cinnamon buns and placed them in the microwave before she noticed. For some reason, he never seemed to be on Gram's good side.

After pouring both of them their usual morning orange juice, he pulled out the buns and grabbed a cup of coffee.

"I'll take a couple buns, thank you, Logan." His Gram didn't even look at him as she commanded two of the treats.

He didn't say a word, just placed them on a separate plate and set it on the table next to her. There were no more in the fridge, so he pulled out sausage she'd cooked up the night before and added it to the microwave.

Chewing the sticky sweet bun while he leaned against the counter, he watched his daughter's facial expressions. She smiled more than she fussed, which was a big change compared to nine months ago. Her face lit up as she grasped a small spoon and stuffed her mouth with oatmeal. He noticed her wince as the spoon hit a sensitive spot. "I think she's cutting another tooth."

She pointed the spoon at her great-gram. "More."

"Then put it in the bowl, Char." His grandmother pointed to the oatmeal and Charlotte looked at it as if it appeared out of nowhere. A wide smile split her lips, showing a bottom row of teeth. A squeal preceded the spoon being thrust into the bowl and it skidding halfway across the tray.

Gram patiently moved it away from the edge when Charlotte stuck the spoon in her mouth again. Her eyes widened this time and watered.

His heart jumped into his throat to know she'd hurt herself.

As if his grandmother knew he was about to comfort his daughter and take over feeding her, she waved him off. "You have chores and a new horse coming. I'll take care of your princess. I don't want her spoiled rotten by the time she's two."

Charlotte's attention had quickly focused on Gram, forgetting her own pain. Only because of that was he able to stuff his warmed-up sausage into a piece of bread and blow his daughter a kiss. "Bye, Charlotte."

"Da-da, bye-bye."

Her chubby little hand dropped the spoon on her tray as she opened and closed her hand at him.

Damn, he loved that child more than his own life. Striding out of the room before he did something his grandmother was sure to scold him for, he headed for the front porch. If she thought Charlotte wasn't spoiled yet, she had blinders on. His daughter was the apple of every family member's eye, mostly his.

Yet she was half Kylie's.

That single thought dispelled all the joy he felt at spending time with his daughter. He hadn't heard a word from Kylie in two days. He'd given her his number, so she could call next time she thought to just show up at the ranch.

His fear was she had hired a lawyer. He may be home all day and have a great support system on this ranch, but a good lawyer would make his life look like the worst possible one for a baby girl to grow-up in and plead mother's intuition and all that. He would do anything to keep that from happening.

He took a seat in one of the chairs on the porch and set his coffee on a small end table, usually used for beers at sunset. Taking a bite of the Italian sausage, he savored the spices before having a sip of coffee. He hadn't heard or seen Jenna either, not even when he went into town to pick up more nails. He'd driven by her office and a number of cars were parked outside on Main Street, so she was probably busy with her animal patients.

Would she talk to him when she came out later or would she ignore him? His hand tightened on the plate he held. He'd make her talk to him. No, he'd show her he could agree with her. Maybe his arguing all the time was why she wanted to talk to Cole. If he stopped doing that, she'd have nothing to complain about. And if being nice led to a kiss, he was certainly good with that.

He took another bite of his impromptu sausage sandwich. Thinking about Jenna calmed him down enough to focus. Trace should be arriving soon and they could get a stall ready for the new horse.

Damn, Cole didn't tell him what was wrong with it. Logan glanced at his watch. Cole would be pissed if he called him while on shift. He'd just have to wait for the horse to arrive to find out what its problem was. Hopefully, it was just the burn scars he heard Cole mention to Jenna.

Every horse that came to Last Chance had a sad story behind it. Cole was great at finding new homes for them once they had overcome any long-term side effects. Some stayed at Last Chance forever, like the horse he rode, Black Jack, who was severely claustrophobic thanks to being buried in an old coal mine.

The horse his brother rode, Lightyear, wouldn't let anyone touch his face. Trace had figured out a way to get a bridle on the horse, but other than Trace, no one could touch its face without it freaking out. Macy's owner had bought her cheap, thinking her facial markings would change. When she grew uglier in her owner's mind, she was put out in a pasture with other horses during heat. The owner was clueless. Of course, she got pregnant and he didn't want to pay to feed her anymore. Luckily, a friend of Cole's heard about the horse and took it off the owner's hands, delivering Macy to Last Chance.

He took another large bite of sausage. Jenna had to give

Macy a lot of shots as her owner was negligent about regular vet visits too. Usually, the horses came through animal welfare. That's how Lacey ended up with Angel, who now resided in a temporary lean-to at her and Cole's new house farther west on the ranch. Since Angel feared all men, it was a better place for her to be than here with him and his brother.

Taking another swallow of coffee, he followed it with the rest of the sausage. Not knowing what the new horse might have for issues made it difficult to prepare for, so he'd get a stall ready, but also have the north corral free just in case. At the sound of horse's hooves, he stood with coffee in hand and walked to the end of the porch.

Trace rode in on Lightyear. When he'd dismounted, Logan called out. "Leave the north corral free. We have a new horse coming today."

His brother nodded before leading Lightyear into the barn.

Taking the final gulp of coffee, he set the cup on the end table then followed after his brother. He'd get Macy and the foal out to the south corral. It was still cool, but the little colt had an abundance of energy that he'd swear was pushing Macy's patience. Maybe he'd move Black Jack out there, too. His horse might like a little company for a change and it would give the colt something new to investigate.

He passed Trace and stepped up to Macy's stall. Sure enough, the foal was bouncing his head up and down. If Logan didn't know better, he'd swear Macy sighed. "Hey little guy, are you bothering mama?"

The colt stopped to look at him then trotted to the door. "Guess you're ready to go. You love this cooler air, don't you?" He turned and headed for the tack room to get a halter for Macy.

When he returned, Trace was waiting for him. "Are you still calling him Charlotte's Horse?" He pointed to the baby colt.

"Yeah." At Trace's look of disbelief, he finally explained. "I'm going to let Charlotte name him."

"Are you starting a pool? I'll put a hundred down on 'Kissie,' but I might switch that to 'No' if Whisper wants to bet on 'Kissie'. Either way we would win."

"No, I'm not taking bets. I'm just hoping it doesn't become da-da." He ignored Trace's laugh and opened the stall door. As he placed the halter over Macy's head, the colt grabbed one lead with its teeth.

"Which stall do you want to use for our new arrival?"

He pulled the lead from the colt's mouth and led Macy out. "The first one on the right as you come in. I think we should have it near the entrance because Cole didn't tell me what to expect."

"Ah, that's why you want the north corral free."

"Yeah." He walked the mare out to the south corral, the foal running beside them, stopping to look at a fence post then bounding back to them. Once he had Macy and the colt inside, he closed the gate and took off the halter. "There you go."

Macy continued to stand there as the colt decided it was the perfect time to nurse. He gave the mare a couple strokes on her neck. "Don't worry. In no time, he'll be grown and you'll wonder where the time went."

Logan left the pair to themselves and headed for the barn. He opened Black Jack's gate and stepped in. "How about a little sunshine, buddy?"

The horse pushed its nose against his hip.

"Will you stop that? I don't have a treat. If you play with Charlotte's Horse, I'll reward you, but not before then." Fitting the halter over the horse, he brought him out of his private stall and led him to the corral.

Once letting Black Jack go, he laughed at the colt, who had

suddenly glued himself to his mama. "Don't worry Macy. He'll be playing out here in no time." He closed the gate and headed back to the barn to help Trace ready the stall.

As irritating as his younger brother's happy attitude could be, he was a worker. Their father had instilled that in them from an early age, yet no matter how hard he'd worked, he'd still lost the ranch. That last year, beef prices had hit the skids due to a glut of beef cattle. Just his luck that most of his herd was ripe for selling and they needed the money.

Now his mom was living in an apartment above her shop in town selling crafts and postcards to tourists just to keep a roof over her head...again because of his luck.

He'd found her a small home not far from town that they could afford with what was left from the sale of the ranch after all the debts were paid, but a bidding war started on the little house. They lost it. In the end, the only place they could afford for her was the shop in town. He hated that she had to work when she should be enjoying life.

"Hey, you going to help or just stand there looking pretty?" Trace grinned at him as he threw a twenty-five-pound bag of pine shavings over his shoulder.

"Right." He strode past his brother and grabbed a couple more bags before entering the stall for the new horse.

"If this new resident is a stallion, we may have trouble with Sampson." Trace nodded toward the stall across the way where Cole's horse stood watching them.

Logan shrugged as he ripped open the bags and started spreading. "We could have problems with it even if the horse is a mare. We should put Tiny Dancer in with Macy, the colt and Black Jack. I'll take Sadie and Sampson out after we get this ready. If Sampson acts up when we bring him back in, you can lead him over to Cole's place."

Trace paused on his way for more bedding. "Why do I see more fence building in our future?"

"As long as Cole helps." He finished spreading the shavings then followed his brother out.

By lunch time, the two of them had the stall ready, Sadie, Sampson, and Tiny Dancer outside, and all the horses fed and watered.

"Cole is going to have to build another barn if he keeps bringing in horses at this pace." He and his brother stood by the south corral watching the colt prance around Black Jack, while Macy enjoyed the shade of the shelter.

He didn't blame her for refusing to budge. The thermometer on the barn was reaching ninety-five and would probably top out around a hundred by late afternoon. Plus, the humidity was up, part of the curse of Monsoon Season. The reward would be the rains, but so far, they'd only had a couple downpours to provide a little relief. It would be helpful if they could get another before October, which signaled the end of the season.

Trace nodded. "I think you're right. Maybe he needs a stable just for those who will stay here for the rest of their lives and one for those who have the possibility of finding a new home."

"That would make it easy to keep track, but it may not work depending on personalities."

Trace chuckled. "You mean for horses like Black Jack?"

"Yeah."

"I'll mention it to Whisper anyway." Trace took his foot off the bottom rail of the fence. "I'm going to take Lightyear home, grab some lunch and bring the truck down. Call me if the new horse shows up before I get back and I'll hightail it down here."

"Will do." Logan kept his eye on the antics of the colt

until his brother rode by on his horse. Technically, Lightyear was Cole's horse, but since Trace was the only one who could get a bridle on the beast and since his girlfriend funded all the horse care now, no one would ever argue with him about it. Not even Cole.

Turning away from the corral, Logan headed for the house. Charlotte would be going in for a nap soon and he wanted to show her the "baby" as she would see it. It was time.

Once inside, he found her in her playpen happily playing with her stuffed teddy and two rubber horses. His grandmother, who was on the phone, watched him like a hawk.

"How's my girl? Do you want to see a baby horsey?"

Charlotte's smile at his voice filled his heart with a happiness he only felt with her. She scrambled to her feet, holding on to the side of her play pen with one hand as she lifted the ever-present teddy over her head. "Up, Da-da. Up."

Ignoring the frown of his grandmother, he lifted his daughter into his arms. "Ready to see the baby horsey?"

"Baby, da-da. Kissie."

He chuckled as he left the family room and strode outside onto the porch. Holding his daughter was like a balm to his soul. Everything wrong with the world melted away when he was with her…and she was smiling.

"Baby." Charlotte's head whipped around as they passed Sampson in his corral.

Logan smiled. "No Sunshine. That's a horsey. That's Sampson, Uncle Cole's horsey."

She turned back to look at him. "Samsam?"

"Yes, Samsam." Cole would love that.

She giggled and smacked her teddy down against his arm.

He stopped at the south corral and pointed to the colt. "Look, Charlotte. A baby horsey."

She turned her head and when she caught sight of the colt, her eyes widened and her face grew serious. Her words were quiet. "Baby horzie."

He swallowed hard. "Yes, a baby horsey."

Spotting them, the young colt bounded toward them, stopping just three feet from the fence. It bobbed its head.

His daughter remained transfixed then lifted her free hand and opened and closed it toward the colt. "Baby horzie." Her voice was soft with wonder.

The little horse stopped moving for a few seconds, then pranced across the enclosure.

Charlotte turned her head to look at him even as she pointed with her teddy bear toward where the colt went. "Baby horzie."

"Yes, baby horsey. Just like baby Charlotte."

Her eyes grew round again and she smiled a toothy grin before batting her chest with her teddy bear. "Baby."

He grinned, blinking at the water in his eyes. "Yes, another baby."

Her head whipped back to find the colt, who stood at the other end of the corral. "Eeeeeee!"

Her squeal of delight shocked both him and the colt, who beelined it back to his mom.

"Okay, enough horsey for today." He turned away, but his daughter looked over her shoulder, leaning over his arm.

Her precarious position forced him to carry her against his chest so she could watch the colt over his shoulder as they walked away, his back being hammered by the teddy as she chanted, "Baby horzie. Baby horzie."

When he made it to the porch, he found his grandmother watching them. "You're going to spoil her."

He shook his head as he walked by her. "Too late."

She sighed behind him. "You can bring her upstairs. It's time for her nap."

Logan carried Charlotte to their bedroom, surprised to see her eyes already closed. Placing her in the crib, he stroked her cheek gently. She'd rearranged his life and taught him so much just by being alive.

His grandmother's hand on his shoulder had him turning around.

"There's a truck coming up the driveway. I think the new horse is here."

He nodded. As usual there would be a lot to learn in a very short time. He left the room quietly and headed downstairs. Before going out, he stopped in the kitchen, following the fresh baked smell of something. On the counter was a plate of blueberry muffins, probably for tomorrow morning's breakfast. Grabbing up two, he peeled back the paper cup of one and stuffed it in his mouth before the screen door closed behind him.

Two people exited a white double-cab pickup truck with a horse trailer. Pulling in next to them was Trace. *Perfect timing brother.* His brother came around the front of his truck to greet the man in a black cowboy hat.

Palming one of the muffins, Logan held out his hand to the woman with wavy black hair. "Welcome to Last Chance."

She smiled. "I'm Dana, the animal rescuer."

Logan widened his eyes before glancing at the chuckling man who came around the front of the truck.

The man held out his hand. "I'm Bo Fletcher, the people rescuer." He was Logan's height, but built more like Cole. Though he wore a cowboy hat, it was obvious he was a firefighter.

"Welcome. Cole said you drove all the way from Dallas to bring us a new horse."

Dana gave Bo a worried glance, then stood straighter and hooked her thumb over her shoulder. "We did. Let me introduce you to Cyclone."

Cyclone? Logan glanced toward the north corral they had cleared. Would that fence hold a horse named Cyclone? Only one way to find out. Following Dana to the back of the trailer he froze.

Well, damn. The horse was a fucking Clydesdale!

Chapter Six

Jenna finished typing in the last of her notes on Mrs. Greyson's orange tabby cat, Marzipan, and saved her file. Picking up her chart of patients for the day, she breathed a relieved sigh to see Connie had left her a half hour for lunch.

Her receptionist was worth her weight in gold. She was thankful every day that Connie had decided to retire early and move to Arizona only to get bored within a month's time.

If Connie hadn't found the litter of feral kittens and brought them to the office the day Jenna had been overrun with appointments, she probably would have never found the time to hire anyone. She'd been managing with just herself and a part-time vet tech up until then.

Putting down the chart, she headed out to the front. There was a good chance Connie had already ordered their lunch from one of the three eateries nearby and all Jenna would have to do is pick it up. When she reached the waiting area, there was no one there except Mr. Erickson's dog, Butterball.

The dog wagged its tail at her but didn't move as it was well trained and was probably told to sit by its master.

"Come here, Butterball."

The English Bulldog immediately waddled over to her and licked her hand.

When the restroom door opened, Connie came out. "I ordered lunch from Ollie's."

"Great. Where's Mr. Erickson?"

Connie's smile disappeared. "The poor man. He passed away. His son said he had an aneurysm. By time the ambulance arrived, it was too late."

She stood. "I'm very sorry to hear that. He was such a nice man. So why is Butterball here?"

"It was Mr. Erickson's wish that you have him."

"Me?" Her schedule was far too crazy for her to own an animal unless it was a farm cat that fed and watered itself and didn't need any attention.

Connie pinned a loose blonde strand back into her upswept hair-do then gave her a long look. "Yes, *you*. I'm sure Mr. Erikson told you that you needed a companion or at the very least a watch dog. I know he told me that many a time."

Darn, the older man *had* said that, but she thought he meant she should get a dog, not that he wanted her to have his. "But what about his son? Wouldn't he want Butterball?"

"He already has three little dogs and said if he brought home one more his wife would divorce him."

"I can't believe she'd do that with it being his dad's dog."

Connie nodded her head. "I can. That woman has a mean streak if you ask me. My friend knows that woman's mother and the stories I've heard would curl your toes."

She should have known Connie knew someone who knew someone. The woman had made it her mission in life to be the 411 for the entire town.

"Now go get our lunch while you still have time to eat

yours. I'm sure Butterball would enjoy the walk." Connie picked up a leash and set it on the counter.

She could stand here and argue with her receptionist or take the dog and pick up lunch while it was still hot because when Connie ordered from Ollie's it was always the special of the day, which was invariably a warm dish.

Taking the leash, she attached it to Butterball and left. Luckily, the dog was very well behaved and known to at least half the town, so when she tied him to the post of the porch at Ollie's, he had plenty of attention while she went inside and paid.

As she walked him back to her office, she gave him time to pee on a small cactus before heading inside. He may be a very well-trained dog, but she'd have to find someone else to give him to. Her life was far too busy for a dog, especially a four-year-old English Bulldog who was used to being an only child.

Setting the lunch on the counter, she unhooked Butterball and handed the leash to Connie. "I'll take this in my office. What is it, by the way?"

Connie grinned. "My favorite, chicken pot pie."

Jenna's stomach growled in response and Connie shooed her away with a wave of her hand. "You go eat. I've got things covered here."

Gratefully, she brought her lunch to her office and opened it up, cutting into the crust to let the hot aroma escape so she wouldn't burn her mouth. As she sat, she looked down to find Butterball at her feet. "If you think you're getting some, you are sadly mistaken. I'm a vet. I know exactly what you can and can't have and this is not for you."

The dog looked at her with imploring eyes, but he finally decided she wouldn't be moved and laid down at her feet.

She was glad because in about three more seconds she

would have caved. Now, if she could just hold out long enough with Logan until she could quit the Last Chance, she'd be golden.

Taking a bite of the delicious pot pie, she glanced at the clock and did a quick calculation. In five and a half hours she could finally tell Cole the news then check the new horse and be done. Maybe she'd get lucky and the man who owned half her heart would be meeting with his baby's mother.

As her lunch cooled, she ate faster and faster, her gaze flicking between Butterball and the clock on her wall.

Connie stuck her head in. "Your one o'clock appointment is here. I put them in exam room two."

"Thank you." She picked up the schedule. They always used exam room two just for cats and it appeared there would be more than one. Miss Knox had brought four of her cats for their annual vaccinations.

Jenna stood and almost tripped over Butterball. "I can't bring you in with me, honey. You'll have to stay in here. Stay."

The dog, who rose to his feet when she caught her balance, lay down again at her command. She wished she had that kind of control over her own heart. Heading for the exam room, she forced herself to focus on the work she loved.

It turned out to be a busy afternoon and in no time Connie was saying goodbye and heading out to her weekly poker game. Jenna called Butterball from behind the reception desk where she found him halfway through the afternoon. "I think Connie wants to keep you here, that's what I think."

She hooked his leash and turned out the lights. "You ready to check out a horse ranch?"

Butterball wagged his tail while she locked up then he followed her to her car. When she opened the driver door, he hopped in and settled himself on the passenger seat. "Oh, really?"

He looked at her innocently.

"That's not a safe place for you. In the back, BB."

He blinked as if he had no clue what she meant.

She squinted her eyes at him and pointed to the back seat. "Butterball. Back."

His ears lowered and he crawled between the seats to lay across the back.

"Good dog." She settled in and quickly had them headed toward Last Chance. As she drove closer, her grip on the wheel tightened. After a sleepless night of Logan making love to her all over again, she'd finally made up her mind. Yet even as she prepared to tell Cole the news, her gut tightened. Not only would she no longer have the much needed income, but she wouldn't be seeing Logan again unless in passing.

But that's why she was quitting as the ranch's vet, so she wouldn't see him anymore—to go back to the way it was after the county fair last year. No, it wasn't just like that at all because Logan had stopped yelling at her and taken to kissing her again. How was she supposed to forget about him if he did that?

She slowed as she came to the dirt-packed yard of Last Chance. An empty horse trailer was parked to the left, and she pulled up next to it. Maybe she could sneak into the barn, check out the new horse, and leave without anyone knowing she'd been there. The only problem with that plan was she needed to find Cole.

The lights were on in the house and a yellow glow spilled out onto the porch, but no one was in the living room. Exiting her car, she grabbed her bag and almost forgot about Butterball. He'd probably like to stretch his legs after the ride, but she had no idea how he would react to horses.

Mr. Erickson lived in a small development with equally small houses. Butterball had probably never even seen a horse.

She opened the back and hooked the leash on him as he wagged his tail. "Okay, come on."

As they approached the barn, she listened intently. Not hearing any voices, she brought Butterball near Black Jack's outdoor stall. Butterball immediately barked.

"Shh, we don't need everyone to know we're here."

The dog sat on his haunches and stared at Black Jack. Luckily, the horse decided to investigate the barker.

She held on tight to the leash in case Butterball misbehaved or Black Jack decided to show his teeth.

"Don't worry. Black Jack likes dogs."

Damn, she knew that low voice. She snapped her head around to find Logan leaning against the entrance to the barn, his long, jean-clad legs crossed at the ankle, his black cowboy boots covered in dust, and his enigmatic hazel eyes studying her. "That's good. I don't think Butterball has ever met a horse before."

His brow raised. "Butterball?"

"I didn't name him." She turned back to the dog in question to make sure he was behaving, but it was clear she needn't worry. He'd jumped his front paws on to the steel rail and played noses with Black Jack.

She returned her gaze to Logan. "You know anyone who would like a well-trained English Bulldog?"

This time Logan frowned. "You're giving your dog away?"

"I'm not sure he qualifies as *my* dog. I just inherited him this afternoon." She pulled on Butterball's leash, but he fought her.

"You can tie him up right there." Logan's voice came from way too close and she stepped back. He had come up behind her without a sound.

She turned her back and tied Butterball to the post. Then

she picked up her bag and strode past the one person she'd hoped she wouldn't see. The barn lights were on and she found the Clydesdale in the very first stall. Her heart lurched at the sight.

He had once been a beautiful horse, but now he had burn scars over his back and down one side. "You poor baby."

Logan followed her. "This is Cyclone. He was in a barn fire and the woman inside the house is the one who threw a blanket on him and saved him from burning to death."

Her breath caught at the courage that had to have taken, but she tensed as well at the admiration in Logan's voice. What did she care if there was yet another woman he liked. "He was a lucky horse."

"If you want the full story, Dana is inside with Bo. They're friends of Cole's from Dallas."

Her tension eased but she mentally kicked herself for being jealous when her whole point in sneaking out to the barn was to avoid any kind of conversation with Logan. She was so messed up around him.

"Excuse me." She looked at him to make him move his arm which blocked her access to the stall.

"Wait. You need to know that Cyclone has a habit of kicking."

Was that why he was out in the barn? Waiting for her so he could warn her? She tapped down her gratefulness and pulled out the tools of her trade. "Does he kick at any particular time or for a particular reason?"

Logan shook his head. "None that Dana could tell. I thought you might want to ask Whisper if she could figure it out."

She frowned. "Why don't you ask Trace to ask her? He sees a lot more of her than I do." Fudge. That came out wrong.

Logan's lip quirked. "I hope so, but I'm not sure she takes Trace's requests as priority."

He needed to *not* smile. She couldn't resist his smile. "Okay, I will, and you can consider me duly warned. Now, I need to do my job."

His almost-smile disappeared as he opened the stall door for her.

"Other than kicking and his scars, is there anything else I should know about this horse?"

Logan shrugged. "His paperwork is in the house. It has all his vaccines listed on it, so you should probably look at it before prescribing anything."

In other words, instead of sneaking into the barn, she should have knocked on the door and looked at everything first. *Busted.* "I'll do that."

Slipping into the stall, she introduced herself to Cyclone. She'd never checked over a Clydesdale before as there weren't any in the area, but she did brush up on them before coming to the ranch. Cole had started a habit of letting her know what he could about every horse before she came to examine it.

"Hey, Cyclone. You're a sweet boy." The horse stepped toward her and pushed her hand with his nose. "I don't have any treats for you boy, though I'm sure you deserve them."

She patted the horse's neck and looked over his scars. They were healing well, a light pink in color that would probably fade to a grayish-white color eventually. No hair would ever grow back there, which meant he may need a light, soft blanket this winter. Luckily, Clydesdales were usually good in the cold. Whatever vet took care of Cyclone must have had a strong stomach. Even now, with the scars doing well, she had to move to his other side for a break from the sight.

Crouching down near his front legs, she kept well away

from a front kick and inspected the feathering around his feet. Keeping that clean was a tough chore and one Cole may not have fully realized. She inspected for signs of "the itch" that the breed was known for contracting.

She continued around the horse before returning to his head to inspect his teeth. Clydesdales were known for being docile animals, but even so, she had to swallow hard as she examined his mouth. He was the largest and tallest horse she'd ever worked with. She patted him on the neck again. "You are one healthy horse, Cyclone, and we're going to keep you that way."

She carefully stepped around him and exited the stall.

"So?"

Logan spoke from above her as she crouched down to put her stethoscope back in her bag. "So, he's very healthy except for the burns, but they are healing well. Whoever treated him, did everything right. His feet look good, but that feathering needs to be kept free of mud which is high maintenance. He has no signs of the itch, which is good and his heart is strong. I'll have to check his chart to see where he is with vaccinations and any past issues."

When she stood again, Logan stepped closer. "Why didn't you go to the house first?"

She could lie, but what good would that do? "I was hoping to avoid you."

He looked over her head and sighed. "I don't want you to feel uncomfortable around me."

"I guess you don't always get what you want then."

Logan barked a cynical laugh before meeting her gaze. "If I got what I wanted, I'd still own Ragged Peaks ranch and my dad would be riding the fence line with me instead of being six feet under." He turned away from her and took a step toward the barn entrance.

She'd struck a nerve she didn't know was there and she would have to be a piece of quartz to not be effected by his reaction. She grabbed his arm to stop him. "I'm sorry. I thought you sold your ranch because you wanted to. I didn't know about your dad."

He halted when she touched him and didn't move as if frozen in his own anger and sorrow. Defeat emanated off him in waves.

She wanted to take away his pain, but self-preservation kept her silent.

Finally, he looked at her over his shoulder. "My dad…my dad and I were best friends. Then he had a stroke and…When I buried him, I…" He swallowed. "I sold the ranch to pay off the debts, moved mom into a place in town with what was left and came here with Charlotte."

At the mention of his daughter, the sharp angles in his face softened a hair. Maybe no one else would notice that, but she did. "I think you made the right decision. This is a beautiful place to raise a child."

He turned to face her, dislodging her hand from his arm. "It is. It's my last chance to get it right."

The self-loathing in his voice pulled at her heart. It was said misery loved company, so she gave him a half-hearted smile. "You should see the family homestead I'm living in. It hasn't been repaired in twenty years. What's left of the barn wouldn't keep the weather out if I could afford the time or cost to have animals, and my school and veterinarian practice debts are keeping me from doing anything about it. I'd say between the two of us, you've made better decisions than I have."

He shook his head. "No, I've had a string of bad luck followed by bad decisions." His gaze grew intense, appearing dark gray in the light of the barn. "One of those bad decisions was never calling you back after our night together."

Her breath caught in her chest and circled around her heart, squeezing it hard. "Why didn't you?"

He didn't look away. "I knew if I did I would kill whatever it was we had. That one day and night was perfect and for the first time since my dad died, I was happy." He cracked all the knuckles at once on his right hand by squeezing his fist in his left one. "But the following day my mother and I went to the bank to take out a loan. Cattle prices had fallen and we couldn't pay everyone. The bank wouldn't give us one."

His gaze moved past her to another time. "We decided to sell. My luck was running true to form and we only had one offer. We had to take it. Suddenly, I was a father and homeless. I couldn't call you. I preferred you think you were another one-night-stand to me and know that with me there was no future."

She wanted to yell at him that he was an idiot, she could have helped somehow, but deep down, she recognized it for what it was, her own wish to be with him. "Then you moved here and found out I was the vet."

His lips quirked up on one side. "Yeah. More bad luck. You could see for yourself I was a failure and with a kid, no less."

Her own hurt melted at his confession. In his ridiculous alpha male thinking, there was no other way to handle seeing her again except to argue with her. "Did you ever think that maybe you needed to look at your situation from another angle?"

He lowered his brow. "What other way is there to look at it? Those are the facts."

"Yes, but the fact that Charlotte was dropped on your doorstep should be looked at as one of the luckiest days of your life. She is the center of your world and without her, you'd probably be a hand on someone else's ranch instead of here, living with family and helping a good cause."

He took a step closer, his height dwarfing her, but she

wasn't intimidated. In fact, her pulse sped at the look in his eyes. "In your version of things, I should be happy that you came back into my life, so I could do what I wanted to do last year."

Her heart skipped as he lowered his head. "What was that?"

"Keep you." His words came out in a whisper just before his mouth lowered and he gave her a sweet kiss. One filled with tenderness, not passion.

She raised her hands to his chest, her defenses going up even as her heart softened.

He raised his head, gazing into her eyes. "Jenna."

"What are you saying Logan?"

"You already know I'm no good with words. I'm better with action, doing, feeling. I want you in my life again."

She clamped her jaw down hard to keep from yelling "yes." What was she thinking? "Okay, so what does that mean?"

"I don't know. Can we just take it a day at a time?"

Disappointment rifled through her, which was stupid. What did she expect, a marriage proposal? She obviously didn't think very well around him. She stepped back, out of his arms to put a little space between them, even if it was just physical space. "Okay, I think I can live with that for now."

Logan smiled, showing his white teeth which contrasted sharply against the dark stubble around his lips. As he stepped toward her again, she grabbed up her bag from the floor and headed for the exit.

"Wait." Logan blocked her way. "Where are you going?"

She frowned at him, anything to keep away the physical need that built inside her. "I'm going home. It's late." She pointed to Butterball who had laid down next to the fence and fallen asleep. "I have to feed him and myself."

Instead of building space between them, her words seemed

to challenge him. He stepped closer, or rather stalked closer because as she backed up, he followed until her back was against the empty stall across from Cyclone.

"Logan." She used her best authoritative tone on him, but it didn't work.

He put a hand on either side of her, trapping her against the wall. "Stay."

She swallowed at the desire in his eyes. "I—"

His mouth came down on hers and this time there was nothing sweet about it. Though he didn't touch her anywhere else, his tongue held her in place as he tasted her fully.

She dropped her bag and grabbed a hold of his shirt as weakness filled her, excitement building in her abdomen. When his kiss moved from her mouth to the side of her neck, she felt herself caving. Then what? "Logan, stop."

His lips froze just beneath her ear. He remained there a few seconds before pulling back to look at her. "What's wrong?"

She licked her lips as she tried to find the right words. "I'm no good at this. I can't make love with you one night and pretend it never happened."

He frowned. "That's not what this is, or what it would be. I haven't slept with another woman since the night we were together."

Her gut tightened as hope rose. "Are you trying to tell me you've been faithful to me?" She crinkled her brow in disbelief.

He smirked. "I guess you could say that." His smile disappeared. "I admit that before I met you I only slept with women one time. It wasn't meaningless, but it also wasn't meaningful. I didn't want to start a relationship. Before my dad had his first stroke, I spent my days working with him. Afterwards, it was the ranch and him and mom. There was no room in my life for a girlfriend." He paused.

As she waited for him to continue, she tried to crush the sweet feeling bubbling up inside her.

"Then I met you. There was so much about you I liked. You were intelligent, pretty, down-to-earth and you didn't try to be someone you weren't with painted nails, dyed hair and clothes that were too tight. You were just you. After that night, I wasn't attracted to anyone and Charlotte took over any free time I had."

So, she made an impression, but it could also be he just didn't have time…in a whole year? "Let me get this straight. You haven't had sex with anyone in over a year?"

He shook his head. "No."

Wow. She hadn't either, but that was no surprise. That Logan Williams, Mr. Stud, hadn't, threw her off balance.

"Let me make love to you. I promise I won't disappear again."

She swallowed. Though one side of her was telling her to run, she was weak, especially in the face of his serious gaze. She gave him half a smile. "Will you promise to call me in the morning?" Though she'd said it to lighten the mood, she held her breath for his answer.

"I promise."

A strange feeling of relief swept through her as if her heart was protected, though that made no sense.

"Jenna?"

She gave him a half nod, expecting a triumphant smile, but it didn't come. Instead, his gaze became more intense and he cupped her face in his hands. "I've dreamed of making love to you for months. I remember every inch of you and I cannot wait."

Before the desire his need caused could fully settle in her belly, his mouth came down on hers in an almost frantic kiss.

Her body burst into flame and she wrapped her arms

around his neck, pulling herself against him as his tongue tangled with her own. He grasped her ass and pushed her up, urging her to wrap her legs around his waist. She complied, locking her ankles behind him.

As his tongue conquered her mouth, she felt her entrance moistening. Her body remembered him and was anxious for fulfillment. She couldn't help but tighten her legs and squeeze him hard.

His mouth came away. "Damn, I need you." Without another word, he walked into the empty stall and sat her down on a stack of hay bales. He reached behind him and unlocked her legs, stepping away by ducking out from under her arms.

Before she could question why, he had pulled his shirt off over his head. Buttons pinged as they tore from the fabric.

Oh, sweet, delectable, fudge. Logan's chest looked even more massive in the barn's brighter lighting, and since there was no sweat or hay particles sticking to it, it was too enticing not to touch.

As he stepped back to her, she reached her hand out to touch his mounded pectoral, but he grasped her wrist and pulled it around his neck. "Hop on again."

Having no choice, she looped her legs around him, the heat of his chest now warming her own. She pressed herself closer, loving the feel of her breasts giving way to his hard chest.

Logan set her down again, only now his shirt was under her. He unhooked her hands from around his neck. "Too many clothes." His words came out on a growl and he dropped to one knee. Without a word, he pulled off her boots.

When he stood, she didn't hesitate. "I agree." She yanked on his belt buckle and succeeded on the first try. Her feeling of triumph was short lived as he grasped her hands and pulled them away.

He let go to work the buttons on her shirt and she let him, anxious to feel his hands on her skin. He spread her shirt and pulled it down her arms to her wrists, before letting it go only to unhook her front-closing bra, his rough knuckles brushing the sides of her breasts.

Logan didn't slow down. There was no worshipping this time. No soft kisses as he removed each piece of clothing, and she was thankful. Pushing her bra straps down to where her shirt rested at her wrists, he turned his attention to her breasts.

"Damn." Logan's simple word as he gazed at her hard nipples was her only warning before he held both breasts within his hands, massaging them, making her hotter. He lowered his head and holding one breast up, his mouth closed over her entire areola to suck gently.

She moaned as she tried to reach for his head, but her hands were still caught up in her clothes. When his teeth found her nipple and rolled it, she gave up trying to touch him and leaned back against the wall, happy to enjoy the pings of need traveling to her core.

Logan pulled his head back only to nibble at her lips while his thumbs and fingers pinched her hard nubs.

"Logan, please." Her words came out raspy, revealing how much she wanted him, but she didn't care.

He unbuttoned and unzipped her jeans and helped her get them out from under her butt and off one leg, but that's as far as he got. "I have to taste you again."

His hands pushed her thighs farther apart, and he lowered his head. With one hand, he pulled her panties to the side while his other moved to run a finger over her mons, against her clit and down to stroke her opening.

She held her breath as she waited for his next touch.

Chapter Seven

Logan's tongue hit her clit, and she whimpered, her need building. With an expertise she preferred not to think about, he stroked her hard nub, flicking his tongue rapidly until she moaned then stopping to lave it, flooding her sheath with wetness.

When he started his rapid tongue movements again, she tightened just before his finger penetrated her opening and thrust in. Her hips came up. She took his long finger in as far as it could go, her body ready for release.

His finger began to withdraw and thrust while his tongue made love to her clit with strokes and taps alternating, her body reaching a pinnacle of pleasure before she exploded.

Flashes of light played before her closed eyes as she rocked with ecstasy, her sheath flooding with her juices.

Logan's tongue stopped and his finger left her, which made her groan at the loss. Then she felt his tongue thrust into her. Her body jumped to life all over again as he tasted her release.

When he pulled away, she opened her eyes to find him gazing at her, his own need obvious.

He leaned his forehead against hers. "I'm so hard. I don't think I can wait any longer."

His desire for her sent a thrill through her chest. "Then don't."

Logan's body seemed to energize at her words. Unzipping his own jeans, he pulled them and his white underwear down.

Jenna's breath caught in her throat. Logan's rigid cock was bigger than she remembered and more than ready to slide into her.

As he ripped open a condom that he produced from out of the thin air, a seed of doubt crept into her brain. Did he plan on this? Was it a lucky guess? Or was he always prepared? But before she could focus anymore on that, Logan held his cock in his hand and stepped forward. He waited for her to raise her gaze to his.

"Are you sure?"

All her doubt melted away at his simple question. "I'm sure."

He pulled her to the edge of the haybale, his shirt beneath her butt helping to keep the hay from being too prickly. She shook off her shirt and bra straps, freeing her hands.

"You are so beautiful." His gaze had moved to her spread legs where he had pulled her panties to the side again to expose her entrance. She felt her cheeks flush at his compliment. Then he moved his other hand to her thigh, holding it wide.

Her sheath tightened in anticipation. "It's been a long time for me, too."

His gaze flicked to hers for a second as if to confirm she wasn't joking, but then he focused on her clit and she forgot to think at all. His fingers stroked over her hard pleasure point this time, wetting it with her own moisture, tightening her insides all over again.

A deep groan issued from him before he set his cock against her opening.

He pushed inside.

As each inch glided into her, her body stretched to

accommodate him. When he'd gone as far as he could go, she tilted her pelvis to feel him dive even deeper. She moaned loudly, unable to believe he'd finally filled her.

He leaned over her, forcing her to fall back against the stall wall. As he latched onto to her breast with his mouth, he rubbed his pelvis against her clit, his pubic hair stimulating it and making her grasp him hard. His teeth bit at her nipple, causing pleasure to travel from her breast to her filled pussy, sending her closer to the edge without him even moving.

The tickle of another orgasm pulsed close and she arched into his mouth.

As if they had been lovers for years, he let go of her nipple and grasped her thighs, pushing them wide. In the next instant, he pulled out and thrust back in.

Her eyes closed again as Logan pumped into her, holding her thighs in place and slamming against her clit with every thrust. She rocked with him, her breaths growing shallow as her body tightened, preparing to orgasm.

"Oh fuck." Logan's exclamation triggered her release and ecstasy swept over her.

Where they joined, pleasure erupted and all feeling radiated from there. She locked on to his wrists with her hands, holding on as his cock rocked into her, sending new waves of satisfaction through her.

Then he came, his yell spiking her joy, making it complete.

Logan couldn't stop. His orgasm was too strong. Luckily, despite her height, Jenna was no delicate flower, and he pumped into her every drop of bliss barreling through his body.

As he took in deep breaths to calm his racing heart, he gazed at her, enjoying the view of her rosy cheeks and plumped lips from his kisses. Moving his hands from her thighs to her back, he brought her against him, loving the feel of her arms wrapping around his waist.

Everything about her felt right, right now. He didn't want to think beyond the moment.

She lifted her head from his chest. "Isn't that better than arguing with me?"

He chuckled. "I'll have to think about that."

Her smile immediately turned in to a scowl. "You're riding on a wild bronco if you think—"

He tipped her head up and kissed her thoroughly before grinning at her. "It was a joke. If you'll be around me more often, you may want to get in tune with my humor."

She moved one of her hands from his back and pinched his nipple.

"Hey, that hurts."

She smiled innocently at him. "If you're going to be around me, you'll have to get used to what I think is funny and what's not."

He grimaced. "Got it."

She appeared pacified, but when she moved her mouth to the same nipple, he tensed.

"I'm just kissing it to make it feel better."

Her tongue circled it before she gently laved it. Damn, that did feel good.

She pulled her mouth away and looked up at him from beneath her dark lashes. "Do you have anything else that needs to feel better?"

His heart lurched. This was a side of Jenna he hadn't seen since the day they met. Sweet, vulnerable. He felt privileged… and protective. That was new. "Holding you makes everything better."

She rolled her eyes. "Now that I doubt."

"You won't be doubting after tomorrow morning when I call you to wake you up."

Her face softened before she looked away. "You better not. I don't have to get up until—"

A loud crash in the stall across from them made them both freeze. Logan's first thought was that they were still connected and in no position to protect themselves.

Another loud bang made it clear the noise was hooves hitting the stall door.

"Cyclone." Jenna pushed at him to move away.

"Whoa, hold on. He's not going anywhere. That door is sturdy enough."

She sighed. "I'm sure it is, but I don't want him to hurt himself. Besides, we're done here."

He finally gave in and pulled out of her, irritated that she was so anxious to run to a horse. Her face showed a similar let down when he left her, which made him feel a little better. She was just dedicated and as she said, they were done…for now.

She dressed quickly, while he disposed of the condom he'd been carrying in his wallet since the night at the bar. He wanted to make love to her then, but didn't have any on him, not that that had worked out so well anyway.

A louder crash sounded as he stepped into the main section of the barn just in time to see the stall door fly through the air toward Jenna.

Fuck. He threw himself over her just before the door slammed in to his back, the metal latch hitting him in the side and knocking the breath out of him. They fell to the floor. Adrenaline had him kicking the door off them and rolling them away in case Cyclone decided to trample them.

He kept her from the horse and looked over his shoulder. The damn thing just stood there looking at them. A nicker from two stalls down caught the Clydesdale's attention and he walked by them to investigate.

Since it was temporarily safe, he loosened his arms and scanned Jenna's face for injuries. "Are you alright?"

She blinked before nodding. "I think so." She scooted out from under his arm and stood, brushing off her clothes while keeping her eye on the giant horse. "I thought that door was going to hit me. I can't believe how fast you are. Thank you."

Logan pushed himself up to a sitting position. "Fuck." He grabbed his ribs.

Jenna immediately crouched next to him. "What's wrong? Are you hurt?"

He gritted his teeth, and she helped him stand, unable to keep his groan silent. "I think I might have a couple busted ribs."

"Let me see." She pulled on his arm.

"No. I'll be fine. Just get me my shirt…please."

She looked about to argue, but finally walked past him toward the stall they had used. He lifted his arm three inches before the pain hit hard. Damn, just his luck. He'd broken his ribs once before, on the other side and he was one hundred percent sure at least two were cracked.

Jenna came back with his shirt. "Will you at least let me help you put it on?"

He glanced at Cyclone who appeared to be flirting with Tiny Dancer. He could *almost* forgive the boy if that had been his reason for busting out.

Assured Cyclone was otherwise engaged, he nodded and let her help him dress, thankful he didn't have to button his own shirt, though there were only three buttons left on it. He never thought he'd be happy to have a woman *dress* him.

"Damn, I won't be able to dress Charlotte in the morning."

Jenna finished the last button and stepped back. "You

get your daughter dressed in the morning? I thought your grandmother did that."

He started to shrug until a stabbing pain took away his breath for a second. "No, I do it. After all, she *is* my daughter. I don't leave her care to everyone else." The minute he said the words, he sensed Jenna withdraw though she didn't actually move.

"Except now you have Kylie to help."

For a few blissful moments, he'd forgotten about Kylie and what he saw as a threat to the life he'd started with Charlotte. "I haven't heard from her in two days. I'm hoping she just goes away."

Jenna shook her head. "That's not going to happen. She's a mom. She'll be back. I guarantee it." She moved to his side. "Now let's get you to the house. You're going to need a doctor."

He wanted to deny both her claims, but he couldn't. He stared at the stall door. "Yeah. Damn door."

Jenna tsked. "I don't think the door was a willing participant. The big guy over there is to blame. I'll give Whisper a call as soon as I get home. Do you think the woman who brought Cyclone here can get him back into a stall?"

He nodded as he walked with her. "Probably. She said she was an animal rescuer when I met her and she's been taking care of him for over a year now."

"Good. I'd hate to see him hurt himself." Jenna spoke to Butterball, who had woken at all the noise. "I'll be right back for you. You've been such a good boy."

They continued across the dirt yard toward the house. Jenna held his arm on his good side. He didn't really need her, but it was nice to be fussed over. "Do you want to bring him inside with us?"

She shook her head. "I'm not coming in. I have to introduce him to my house since he'll be with me temporarily. I hope I can find a good home for him."

He stopped before taking the steps to the porch. "You're not going to keep him?"

"My life is too busy. It wouldn't be fair."

"Why not just take him with you. He seems well behaved. I know he's just a dog, but when I found Charlotte on my front step, I could have easily turned her over to the police or put her up for adoption without ever checking her DNA. I'm glad I didn't because she has changed my life, changed me. I think Butterball could do the same for you."

She chuckled. "You're right. He's a dog not a child. Now up you go."

He sucked in his breath between his teeth as he put weight on his leg to take the first step. Fuck that hurt. He stalled. "Will you be back tomorrow to look over Cyclone's paperwork?" He couldn't care less about the horse, but confirming that Jenna came back was a high priority for him now.

"Yes, but it will have to be after work again. I have two ranch calls in the morning and appointments all afternoon. Now, come on, just two more steps."

Reassured she'd be back, he gritted his teeth and took the next two steps like a man, as his dad would say. When they reached the door, Jenna opened it for him.

"Earlier you were offering kisses to make me feel better. Think you can spare one now? I could definitely use one." He gave her a self-deprecating smirk.

She frowned before letting the door close in front of him and turning away.

That wasn't the reaction he'd hoped for.

Jenna grabbed the end table he'd used for coffee in the morning and stepped on it. "Number one rule in the medical field is do no harm. This way you won't have to bend over."

Hell, his woman was damn smart. Stepping up to her, he

cupped her face with his free hand and touched his lips to hers. She responded with equal sweetness before her tongue shot into his mouth and ramped him up all over again.

By time he finished tasting her, he was ready to take her to his bed, except in his condition, he was afraid it would be more pain than pleasure.

"Pleasant dreams, Logan." She grinned at him before jumping down from the table and opening the door for him again.

Inside, he could hear laughter coming from the kitchen. As inviting as it was, he'd give anything to stay outside with Jenna without cracked ribs. Thanks to her, his night was bound to be restless.

Unwilling to let her know how much she'd affected him, he winked. "You, too." He walked through the door, a soft cat call whistle following him that made him laugh, making his diaphragm push against his ribs.

"Ah fuck!" Luckily, the door closing covered up his swear of pain.

~~*~~

Logan watched as his brother pounded in the last new rail on the north corral fence. "Look at him. He's got a serious crush on that Paint."

Trace wiped the sweat from beneath his hat before standing to look at Cyclone. "That's an odd couple if ever I saw one. She can barely walk and he breaks through stalls and fences."

He looked past Trace to see a rider flying down the valley toward them. "I think we are about to find out what his problem is." Logan pointed with his good arm, his left one in a sling to remind him not to move it too much while his ribs healed. That, all thanks to an early morning doctor visit and the doc's refusal to bandage his ribs. Something about them needing to move.

His brother's girlfriend, Whisper, only knew two speeds when it came to horses, stopped and a full out gallop. The gray horse she rode like a wild woman was Spirit, a retired racehorse who never did well on a track but thrived at the ranch.

Trace smiled widely. "Isn't she magnificent?"

Logan purposefully misinterpreted the question. "Yes, that horse flies like the wind."

Trace scowled and moved to elbow him.

He quickly stepped aside. "Hey, I'm not wearing this sling just to remind *me* I'm injured. Watch the ribs."

"I don't have to. Gram has them marinating in the fridge." Trace winked before heading around the corral to meet Whisper.

Logan turned back to look at Cyclone. There was something very odd about the horse. He'd watched last night as Dana and Bo ushered the Clydesdale back into his stall then put up ropes over the opening. Cyclone was still there in the morning. Nothing was busted.

When Trace brought him to the north corral before feeding the other horses, he was fine for about thirty minutes. Next thing they heard were the rails being smashed down, yet Cyclone didn't even step out. Why would he break doors and fences if it wasn't to get out?

As Whisper dismounted and strode over, it occurred to him that he had no idea if Jenna knew how to ride. He looked forward to finding out. The sound of surprise in her voice this morning when he'd called her as promised had made his day. She said she'd come out as soon as her last appointment left. That would probably be in time for dinner. He liked the idea of her having a meal with his family.

"Are you sure Logan isn't antagonizing him?" Whisper's voice was loud enough to be heard across the entire yard.

When he'd first seen his brother falling for her, he'd

threatened her, but after the shootout at her trailer, they'd become more like brother and sister. Unfortunately, that meant slinging bull-crap. "If giving him fresh bedding and a corral all to himself is antagonistic, then the answer to that question is yes."

"I knew it." She gave him a fake scowl, but quickly switched to the problem at hand. "What's his story?" She leaned on the corral fence, setting one foot on the bottom rail, her handgun, "Sal," tucked in the waistband of her jeans.

He shook his head, unable to completely understand someone like her. "We don't know. He was a rescue that one of Cole's friends was taking care of. I'm pretty sure the smashing things had something to do with him not being wanted. Then he was burnt in a barn fire, but has healed well."

"He's big. Never seen a Clydesdale in person. Thought they were only used for that beer company."

Just when he'd started to forget she'd been raised off the grid, something she said reminded him. "He's a draft horse. They use this breed for lots of things."

She nodded as if that was all she needed to know. Then she climbed over the fence into the corral.

"Wait, Whisper!" Trace had been tying up Spirit and ran over as she jumped down and strode toward the horse.

Logan grabbed his brother's arm. "Relax. She knows what she's doing. Isn't that what you told me when she approached Black Jack?"

Trace nodded, but still climbed the fence and shadowed her. His brother was so deeply in love, Logan had to wonder if a wedding would be announced soon. Then again, with those two, they'd probably drive up to Vegas, elope and then tell them all after it was done.

Cyclone caught sight of Whisper and met her halfway. He

was a friendly horse and well-tempered like most Clydesdales, which just made the kicking behavior that much more puzzling.

Working on his cousin's ranch had given him a new appreciation for horses. He'd always valued them, but they had simply been part of his family's cattle operation. Now, he saw them as individuals with their own past...like him.

He turned around to look at Black Jack, happy in his outside stall. He'd take him out for a ride as soon as his ribs healed. Maybe Jenna could ride Sadie. A new warmth filled his chest at the idea. The past year, whenever he thought about her, saw her, or argued with her, all he'd felt was frustration, anger and regret, but now...now it was different. He wasn't even sure why.

"You poor thing." Whisper's words brought him back to the activity in the corral.

"Because of the burns?" He opened the gate and walked inside. "From what I hear, Dana was burned as well, risking her life to save him."

Whisper turned her head and scowled at him before returning her focus to Cyclone. She stroked his nose. "You will get all the attention you deserve here."

He frowned. Whisper spoke to animals easier than to people. "Is something wrong?"

She patted the horse and turned to face him. "Isn't that why you asked Dr. Jenna to call me?"

Damn, he walked right in to that one. "So, what is it?"

She nodded her head toward the gate and he followed her out as Trace opened it for them. Once far enough away to suit her, she kept her voice low. "That big strong horse was ignored. Half the time he wasn't brushed, ridden, or even fed." Whisper's hands balled into fists. "He smashes things to bring attention to himself."

Logan pulled back and stared at her. "What?"

She grabbed him by the arm and pulled him halfway across the parking area before he dug in his heels. "Enough. Just tell me what we need to do."

She faced him. "That animal is used to being considered worthless."

He raised his brow. "He's a damn Clydesdale."

"Whatever. The fact is, whoever owned him didn't think he was valuable. Maybe the stupid owner was afraid of him. It doesn't matter why. What you have to do is make him feel special. Lavish him with attention."

"Excuse me?"

Whisper pointed at him. "You heard me. You need to spoil him. Make him feel like he's an important part of the ranch."

He looked to his brother for help, but Trace just shrugged his shoulders.

"And how am I supposed to do that?"

She threw her hands up. "I don't know. You're the one with horse experience. Give him a job or something. Show him off to everyone who visits. Make him part of some daily routine."

He shook his head. "And if I don't?"

"Then you get to repair stall doors, fence railings and porch steps for a living."

"Porch steps?" He glanced at the house just to make sure the three steps in front were still intact.

Whisper shrugged. "Let's just say it's a possibility."

Logan cracked the knuckles in his left hand. Just what he needed, a temperamental giant horse. He looked at Trace. "We're going to need to come up with plan."

Trace nodded, his smile turning serious for once. "We'll think of something."

Logan felt the tension in his gut lessen. As much as his younger brother was a pain in the ass, he was dependable.

"Who the hell is that?" Whisper had turned toward the dirt road heading to the ranch. "And what the freak are they driving. It looks like a coachwhip on steroids."

Logan smirked at the analogy, even as he stifled a groan. Kylie's red convertible *did* look like the snake Whisper referred to as it took the final turn toward the ranch. His hope was that she was equally non-venomous, but if his luck held true, that wouldn't be the case. How the low-to-the-ground vehicle made it across the steep wash halfway between the house and the highway, was beyond him.

Trace strode toward him and Whisper. "That's Kylie, Charlotte's mother."

"I guess it was too much to hope she'd given up." Jenna's admonishment that he thought that a possibility rang in his ears.

"Given up what?" Whisper looked over her shoulder at him.

"Given up trying to see my daughter." His gut tightened. If Kylie was here, it meant she was willing to meet his terms, or she had a lawyer. He didn't like either option.

As the car pulled to a stop, Logan was pleased that his brother stepped back to stand shoulder to shoulder with him. The family bond between them had grown stronger since their father had passed and at times like these, Logan appreciated it.

Kylie stepped out in a pair of pink cowboy boots, white short-shorts, a pink halter and her straight blonde hair held back in a white scarf. She looked like a piece of cotton candy.

Whisper turned away from the approaching woman. "Jezebel."

He widened his eyes at her before she stepped up to his brother and kissed him on the mouth. Trace didn't hesitate to wrap his arms around her to deepen it.

Logan looked away, meeting Kylie's gaze. She'd stopped at the sight.

Whisper pulled out of Trace's arms. "I have to go. Uncle Joey has an appointment with a barber. Ever since old Billy told him about this lady barber, I'm not good enough to cut his hair anymore, the big flirt. If you're eating dinner here, you better be on guard."

At Whisper's command, Trace nodded solemnly.

Did she think Kylie would take her man?

As the woman walked away, she looked at Kylie, before reaching behind her back to touch "Sal," the warning clear.

Trace chuckled. "Too bad you can't find you a woman like that."

He scowled at his brother before turning to face his fate. "Hello, Kylie."

She continued toward them. "Hi, I'm sorry it took me so long to come back, but I had to work. It's such a long drive out here. I think I might start looking for employment in Wickenburg so I don't have such a far drive."

His heart fell into his stomach at her words. "Does that mean you are ready to meet my terms?"

"Yes." She opened the tiny purse that was slung over her shoulder. "I brought a hair sample and my written intentions."

Fuck. That was not what he wanted to hear. "I won't need the sample. We'll go to the lab together to have our mouth's swabbed." Because he would make sure he was the one who received the results, ASAP.

Her smile faltered. "Us?"

"Yes. It's important that I prove I'm Charlotte's dad as well."

She waved him off. "Oh, I know you are. There was never any doubt. You don't have to go."

"Yes, I do."

She rummaged through her little purse, shrugging as she did so. "Okay. Whatever you want."

What I want is for you to disappear.

"Ah, here it is." She pulled out a neatly folded piece of paper and handed it to him. "I brought what you asked for. My intentions." She presented it to him like a trophy.

He had to force himself to take the paper from her. He palmed the folded square and studied her, her look of anticipation made his gut roll.

"Aren't you going to open it?"

No! I don't care what you want, Charlotte is mine!

She gave him a shy smile. "I think you'll like it."

His stomach held still. Could it be she wanted to leave Charlotte to him with occasional visits? He could live with that. Hopeful now, he opened his hand and unfolded the paper.

Chapter Eight

Dear Logan. I think long and hard about my intenson. I feel bad I left Charlotte that nite and missed her every day. I know I do the rite thing, but I feel bad about it.

I want for our daughter is a family. My intenson is to be a mama to Charlotte and a wife to you like we always should be. We have dreams that nite and I want to make them true.

These is my intensons.

Luv Kylie

He stared in shock. Wife? *No!* He swallowed hard. That was never his dream. He would need a lawyer and a good one. How the hell would he pay for that?

His brother's hand on his shoulder caused him to look up. Kylie smiled at him. He quickly turned toward Trace and handed him the paper. At his brother's widening eyes and scowl, he turned back to Kylie.

She frowned. "That was private."

"On the ranch, nothing is private. I live here with my grandparents, my brother here and my cousin."

Her gaze flitted to the house and back. "All together?"

"All on this ranch."

She seemed to think about that for a moment and it didn't appear she liked it much. "Can I see Charlotte now?"

Fuck. "We still need to get the DNA test."

"Come on, Logan. I'm her mother. At least let me see her. Then we can go get the test. Please."

He didn't like it, but he could hear some court judge calling him hard-hearted and not worthy to be a father. He swallowed down bile. "This way."

As he turned, Trace grabbed his shoulder and he winced at the twist on his ribs. "Are you sure?"

"No." He practically growled the word before striding toward the house.

"Wait." Kylie called after him, but he kept going.

When he reached the door, he paused, his manners forcing him to hold the door open for her.

She scooted past in a cloud of pink and lilac scent.

He hated lilacs. "This way." He motioned down the hall toward the informal family room. Charlotte should be up from her nap and playing in her playpen. As Kylie came to the door, she halted.

He looked past her to see Charlotte crawling onto the sofa next to Gram.

Kylie looked back at him. "I thought she'd be bigger by now."

What? Charlotte was perfect. "According to the doctor, she's long for her age."

Kylie stepped into the room. "Hey baby, can you come to mommy?"

Fury swept through him and he grabbed Kylie's arm, spinning her around to face him. "Don't you dare call yourself her mommy until I decide how to tell her. Understand?" His words were ground out in a low whisper, but from her widening eyes, and nodding head, he was satisfied she understood.

He let go of her arm and fisted his hands, ashamed at the

red mark he'd left behind on her arm. He could hear her now claiming to a judge that he abused her.

She walked closer to his daughter. His grandmother stood as Charlotte's lips moved up into a smile.

He shook his head at Gram, who for once, didn't interfere, but who also didn't move an inch.

Charlotte held up her cowboy teddy bear. "Kissie! Kissie!"

"Look at you. What an adorable outfit." Kylie glanced back at him. "I love the pink dress." She crouched next to the couch. "You have a very pretty dress, baby."

Charlotte thrust the teddy bear in Kylie's face. "Kissie."

"You want a kiss?" Kylie leaned in and gave Charlotte a kiss on the forehead.

His daughter scowled. "No. No. No. Kissie." She thrust the teddy again.

Kylie chuckled. "You give kisses."

Charlotte didn't like that idea either and quickly rolled over onto her tummy and shimmied off the couch to stand with one hand on the furniture. "Mimi, kissie." She promptly let go and plopped down on her butt before crawling around Kylie to his grandmother, who scooped her up.

"Logan, I need to feed her. I expect you to come to the kitchen and explain when you're done here."

He nodded as she whisked his daughter past him and out of the room, Charlotte smiling at him over his grandmother's shoulder.

"She's so adorable." Kylie's eyes were misty with unshed tears.

Guilt rifled through him. "She is sometimes. Other times, she's stubborn and she can yell louder than a screeching bobcat."

Kylie cocked her head. "I've never heard a bobcat. Do you have those out here?"

"Occasionally."

They stood in awkward silence for few moments. Finally, he cleared his throat. "I have to get back to work."

"Okay."

He let her precede him out of the house. Once on the porch, she stopped and faced him. "You didn't tell me what you thought of my intentions."

He looked past her. "No. I didn't. They were not what I expected."

She stepped closer and placed her hand on his chest. "What do you think?"

He took her hand and pulled it away, grasping at anything to delay the inevitable. "I need to know you are, who you say you are."

"Fine." She lifted her chin. "Then you better test that hair or go to the lab with me right now because I'm getting tired of this bullshit."

Her blue eyes flashed. Part of his brain warned him to be patient, to get a lawyer before pissing her off, but his protective side was ready to have her off the ranch and out of Charlotte's life. "I'll drive."

She raised her eyebrows in surprise. "Really?"

Stepping back into the house, he grabbed his keys and let his grandmother know what was happening. She started to ask questions, but he walked out. He may hear about it later, but this was in his daughter's best interests right now.

When he strode outside, Kylie was waiting by her car. "I'm sorry I snapped at you. This is just hard for me. We can do this another time."

"No. Now is good." He opened the passenger door of his truck.

After she climbed in, he closed the door and headed for the

driver's seat. It was the last thing he'd expected to do today, but it was also his last chance to discredit Kylie as Charlotte's mom, and even if he was grasping at straws, he'd take it.

As he started the truck, he noticed Cyclone watching him. Damn, why did he get the feeling he'd be repairing more fence today as well.

~~*~~

Jenna patted Cyclone on his side. "You did great, big guy."

He looked back and nudged her with his nose.

She laughed. "You really are a big baby, aren't you?"

Trace, who leaned against the inside of the corral fence grinned. "According to Whisper, he's even a bigger baby than you think."

"What did she say?" She dropped her empty vaccination syringe into a small bag and gathered up her stethoscope.

"He smashes things to get attention."

Jenna snapped her head to face Trace. "Why would a Clydesdale need to attract attention?"

Trace ambled toward the gate and opened it for her. "Whisper says he was ignored, even to the point of his owner forgetting to feed him."

She slung her bag over her shoulder and strode toward him. "That's a travesty."

"More like a pain in the a—um, butt for us. We have to figure out how to keep him busy and spoiled if we want to avoid having to fix whatever he breaks on a daily basis."

She stepped outside the corral and her gaze went to the parked red convertible for the eighteenth time since she'd arrived. She shouldn't be jealous just because Logan took Kylie to get her DNA tested, but the fact he was with her in the same vehicle had her stomach in knots.

"Do you have any ideas?" Trace closed the gate, pulling her attention back to her job.

A job she'd just finished, so she had no reason to stay. "He's technically a heavy draft horse. Is there anything he can pull?"

Trace chuckled. "Sure. He could probably pull down the whole barn if he wanted."

She rolled her eyes at him and headed for her car. She should find Butterball and leave. So much for seeing Logan. She'd hoped when he said take it one day at a time that it could be a daily effort. Maybe she should lower her expectations.

"Aren't you coming in for dinner?"

She dropped her bag on her back seat. "Dinner?"

"Yes, the meal people generally eat at this time of day. D-i-n-n-e-r."

She squinted her eyes at him. "I know what dinner is."

Trace shrugged. "Just checking. Logan said you were staying for dinner, and Gram planned on it. I have to tell you, if you don't join us, she'll be pretty pissed."

Logan told his grandmother she was staying for dinner? Her mood lightened at that. Was she so pathetic that so little could make her happy when it came to that man? She didn't like that at all. Still, dinner was dinner.

She hadn't brought any dog food with her, but there were a few things Butterball could eat that would hold him over until they went home. "Then I guess I better stay. First, I need to find my dog. This whole ranch experience is new for him."

"Good idea. Last I saw, he was trying to wiggle under the stall door where Macy and Charlotte's Horse are."

"What? And you didn't stop him?" She slammed the car door and started for the barn. She had no idea how mama horse would handle Butterball. The dog had been raised in an

110

apartment in Wisconsin before coming to Arizona. He'd never even seen a horse until yesterday.

"I'm sure he's fine. Be quick. Gram doesn't like it when we're late."

She ignored Trace and switched on the low lights for the barn. At first glance, her new dog wasn't in sight. "Great." Striding for the last stall on her left, she imagined all kinds of scenarios. Butterball stomped to a pulp. Butterball cowering in the corner with Macy hovering over him, teeth bared.

What she didn't expect to see was the reality. She halted in front of the stall. The yet to be named colt lay on the hay, its eyes closed with Butterball sleeping against his side, softly snoring. She moved her gaze to Macy who looked at her with kind eyes before returning to her dinner.

She obviously needed to do a little research on English Bulldogs because she hadn't expected that at all. She may know a lot about the medical side of the species, but it appeared she was lacking in the psychology and habits of it.

Not wanting to disturb the dog, she left him as he was and headed out of the barn. The sound of a truck pulling into the yard had her picking up her pace. It had to be Logan. As she rounded the side, she was just in time to see him helping Kylie out of the truck.

Two emotions hit hard. One, concern, as Logan's left arm was in a sling. Did he hurt his arm as well as his ribs in yesterday's crash? The other emotion was pure green jealousy. It raced through her, stopping her breath and freezing her to the spot.

The two spoke for a few minutes before Kylie placed her hand on Logan's good arm and leaned up and kissed him on the cheek.

Oh no, she wasn't having any of that! She strode forward,

being sure to make as much noise with her boots on the dirt as she could. "Good thing you came back when you did. Your Gram won't tolerate you being late to dinner."

Logan spun, obviously not expecting her. Was that guilt on his face? "Phoenix traffic was backed up thanks to an accident on the 101."

Kylie faced her. "Hi, Dr. Jenna." She linked her arm in Logan's. "We just went for a little errand run."

"We had our DNA tested." Logan was quick to explain.

She frowned. "We?"

Kylie looked up at Logan with adoration. "He wanted to prove to me that he's Charlotte's daddy. Isn't that sweet?"

Jenna gritted her teeth, pasted on a fake smile and nodded. What was Logan doing? If he wanted a relationship with his daughter's mother, why did he tell her he wanted one with her? If he thought he could have both, he was in for a rude awakening.

Logan disengaged his arm from Kylie and opened it toward her car. "I will call you when I receive the results."

She waved that comment away. "No need, I can come back tomorrow and we can start working on our family."

"I won't be on the ranch tomorrow. I have to move some horses. I'll have to call you."

Kylie put her hand to her chest. "Oh, you mean like a cattle drive?"

"Something like that."

Jenna dropped her smile as Logan walked the woman to her car. She'd bet a herd of Holsteins Logan was lying about moving horses. Did she really know him that well, or was it wishful thinking? What did Kylie mean "working on our family"? Had Logan caved to Kylie machinations?

Once Kylie was safely on her way down the dirt road, Logan faced Jenna.

"What was that about a family?" She strode toward him.

He headed for her as well, but he didn't answer her question. As soon as he was within feet of her, she opened her mouth to ask it again, but his own swept down on hers as he pulled her toward him with his good arm and kissed her.

Off guard, she melted into the heat of his kiss, but there was a desperation about it that triggered her rational thought. Pushing away, she found herself abruptly released and Logan holding his side.

Darn it. She'd hurt him. Worry, guilt and jealousy collided inside her and she lashed out. "What was that about? What family is she talking about?"

Logan took a few more shallow breaths before answering. "I hope to God Charlotte doesn't inherit any of that woman's brains because she is loco. She came here today with her intentions written on a piece of paper like I asked."

Jenna stepped back, her heart constricting. "Let me guess. She wants you three to be one big happy family."

He nodded. "I didn't tell her no."

Bile crept up her throat. She was an idiot.

He stepped closer, but she backed up. "What are you saying?"

"I'm saying that I got a hold of Trace while I was at the lab and told him to contact his lawyer from the divorce. His attorney specializes in family law, custody being one of his strong points. I don't want Kylie to suspect that I will be ready to battle her for Charlotte."

"Oh, fudge." Her knees went weak with relief, so she grabbed his good arm to steady herself. "I'm sorry I hurt you. From what I saw…"

Logan's lips twitched. "Does that mean you might actually care about me?"

"What do you think?" She looked at him in complete disbelief that he could be so unsure.

He gave her an actual smile that reminded her of their day at the fair. "I think you do, which makes me a whole lot happier." He wiggled his arm out from under her grasp and took her hand. "Let's go in to dinner."

They entered the kitchen to find Trace and Annette already seated with Charlotte in a high chair next to Annette. Logan guided her to a seat then he sat between her and his daughter.

As they ate Annette's hearty pork chops, mashed sweet potatoes with brown sugar, green beans with almonds, biscuits and chocolate cream pie, she learned that Annette's husband was on a hunting trip in Montana, Whisper was nursing a wounded owl, Cole was on shift at the fire station and Lacey was entertaining Cole's friends at home.

"Wasn't Cole going to build a small stable near his new house?" Jenna addressed the question to Annette, but Logan answered.

"Yes. He wanted to be able to house a few horses there. He's already ordered the lumber. It should arrive any day. I think he should just go ahead and build another large stable. At the rate we're taking in horses that can't leave, we'll need a place just for the permanent residents."

He had to be referring to horses like Angel, Sampson, Tiny Dancer, Black Jack and Cyclone. At the thought of the Clydesdale, an idea formed that might just help the big horse with his problem. "What if you had the lumber dropped off here in the yard and used Cyclone to haul it down the valley to Cole's place. It might take longer, but it would make him feel useful."

Logan stared at her in surprise for a moment before he smiled. There was a new look in his eyes as he gazed at her, almost as if he was proud of *his* woman. She had to be mistaken. He was as shy of commitment as a cottontail was of a rattler.

"That's perfect!" Trace's shout broke the moment. "At least that will give us time to think of other things instead of mending fences."

She forced herself to look at Logan's brother and gave him a polite smile. "It would also be good for him to get some exercise. He obviously hasn't been employed in work and he was built for it."

Annette wiped Charlotte's mouth which was covered in chocolate. "Is he ready for a harness? I saw him out there earlier today. Those burn scars look painful."

Jenna turned toward Logan. "He's healed well on the outside, but he will never grow hair. I think you would need some kind of pad on his back that covers his sides where a harness would lie, and I'd start with a small amount of weight."

Logan pushed away his now empty pie plate. "We have some sheepskin in the tack room that would work, but we don't own a large enough harness. I think the Sanders might have one we could borrow to try it out. I don't want to invest in a harness of that kind until we see how Cyclone feels about the whole idea."

She'd known he cared about horses, but when she'd tried to help them, he'd always argued with her, so she'd assumed he didn't see them as individuals with different personalities. Then again, he'd definitely stepped up when Black Jack needed an outdoor shelter.

Maybe she needed to stop expecting the Logan from the fair or the Logan from when she came to help the horses here. Maybe she needed to simply discover who Logan Williams was now.

He rose then walked behind her. "Someone is ready for

bed." Grabbing up the ever-present cowboy teddy bear and stuffing it into his sling, he then lifted his daughter out of her high chair with his good arm, her eyes closing despite her efforts otherwise. That he'd thought to take the teddy bear for his daughter had her heart melting.

"Would you like to help me put her to bed?" Logan's look was guarded as if he wasn't sure how she would react.

She smiled softly. "I would."

As the tension in his jaw eased, she was glad she'd agreed. If there was one thing about Logan she knew without a doubt, it was that he would protect his daughter at all costs. Did that mean he'd marry Kylie to keep Charlotte?

She pushed the thought away as she stood. He didn't think Kylie a good influence on his daughter, so that would be the last thing he'd do. Besides, Trace had already called his lawyer and left a message about Logan.

Jenna followed Logan out of the room, not unaware of Trace's smile or Annette's raised eyebrows. Their reactions made it perfectly clear how special his request was. When they reached the top of the stairs, they turned left to his and Charlotte's room.

The room was plenty big enough with two twin beds, a crib, a changing table and dressers. Logan laid Charlotte down on the changing table and began to undress her. "Can you pull out a clean diaper from the bottom drawer here?"

She nodded before crouching down to retrieve the diaper. "Do you need this powder too?" She looked at him from her crouch.

"No, she's pretty clean tonight. Just the diaper."

As she closed the drawer, she smiled as she caught sight of Logan's scuffed up cowboy boots before she rose to give the cowboy his daughter's diaper.

He took it and gave her the dirty one. "That goes over there."

She quickly disposed of it, not because she minded the smell, but because she enjoyed watching Logan's calloused fingers gently maneuvering Charlotte's dress off. His hands were so large but so gentle.

"Her pajamas are in the second drawer of that dresser."

Jenna moved to it and opened the drawer filled with pink and purple sleepwear. Did he buy these or did Annette? At the image of Logan in a baby store picking out just the right color jammies for Charlotte, Jenna's eyes misted and she quickly picked out a purple ensemble.

With a confidence born of repetition, Logan soon had his sleeping daughter ready for bed. He picked her up and brought her to the crib. "Do you want to give her a kiss goodnight? It's the only time you can kiss her and not the bear." His smile was crooked and a bit uncertain.

She walked over to him, put one arm around his waist, her other hand behind Charlotte's head, and kissed the sweet-smelling child on the cheek. "Sleep well, little one." Hearing her mom's words spill from her own mouth both surprised and saddened her. She looked at Logan to find him staring at her with enigmatic eyes.

Charlotte murmured in her sleep. "Kissie."

Jenna smiled. "You heard her." Raising herself onto her toes, she kissed Logan on the cheek. The action broke his reverie, and he gently laid his daughter in the crib. He kissed her on the forehead, placed the teddy against her hand and she immediately grasped it.

For a moment, they stood there watching Charlotte sleep, her breathing regular, her face relaxed and innocent. Logan finally moved, and taking her hand, led her out of the room.

She expected him to go downstairs, but instead he continued to the other side of the stairs where another bedroom was situated. She only had a moment to notice it had a large bed in it before Logan turned her toward him and cupped her face.

"You are beautiful, inside and out."

She smirked. "You're not so bad yourself."

His face remained serious as he shook his head. "I've been pretty ugly inside. My father's stroke put me in a tailspin, but I'm straightening out. That little girl in there has a lot to do with that." He gestured with his head. "She makes me want to be a better person. She also shows me what an ass I've been. I'm sorry I never called you back."

She started to shake her head, but he held it still.

"No, hear me out. I'm sorry because it was inconsiderate and hurtful, but I'm also sorry because we could have had so much more time together that I've missed out on."

Her heart raced at his words. Was he going to tell her he loved her? Oh damn, what would she say? Did she love him? Really love him?

"I don't want to miss one more moment with you. Will you stay with me tonight?"

Relief and disappointment whirled through her for a moment before she could steady her thoughts. "What about Charlotte?"

His thumb stroked her cheek gently. "We can sleep in here."

What was she afraid of? Dumb question. She was afraid he'd break her heart again. "I don't—"

Logan stopped her words with a kiss. This one was gentle, loving, persuasive.

Instead of answering him, she wrapped her hands around his neck and enjoyed his mouth on hers. Outside, the sound of a truck approaching the ranch filtered through her pleasure.

At a loud crash right outside the house, she broke away. Logan looked at her with worry before they both turned and ran downstairs. Trace and Annette were already on the front porch.

She stopped in shock. A sleek black pick-up truck had t-boned her little car.

Chapter Nine

Logan strode off the porch ready to deck the drunk that had found his way onto their property. The guy better have insurance because he'd totaled Jenna's little car.

When the driver finally exited, Logan stared in shock.

Dillon Hatcher, Cole's brother, stood there looking like a country singer, complete with rhinestones down his red shirt. He rubbed one hand over his face and strode toward him. "Shit. I don't know what that was."

He frowned. "What what was? Are you drunk, Dillon?"

His cousin stopped and scowled at him. "No, I'm not drunk. I'm fucking pissed, but I'm not drunk."

Logan gestured toward Jenna's car, every protective instinct in him wanting to deck his younger cousin. "Explain. And do it fast."

"I didn't do that on purpose. There was some kind of small boulder in the middle of the driveway and as I approached, it suddenly started to move. It had to be one of those desert tortoises, so I swerved to avoid it." Dillon looked directly at the smashed-in car. "I didn't mean to do that."

"You avoided a tortoise?" Jenna's voice behind Logan had him turning toward her, but then he saw the so called "tortoise" and his anger disappeared. He pointed to the opposite side of the yard from the accident. "Is that your tortoise?"

Dillon turned toward Butterball, who sat near the corral looking at them all and shaking.

"Holy shit. Is that a dog?"

"Butterball!" Jenna ran over and crouched down to soothe the poor thing.

When he turned back to look at Dillon, the man's face was white.

"Hey, no harm done. The dog's okay and the car can be replaced. You do have insurance right?"

Dillon nodded absently. "I can't believe she made me so angry I totaled someone's car and almost killed that woman's pet."

Ah, Dillon had been speeding out here. "Who got you so pissed?"

Dillon finally looked at him. "My mom."

Knowing his Aunt Bev, Dillon was probably in the right, though it didn't excuse the mess he'd made. "Why don't you go inside with Gram and Trace? You're probably going to be sore tomorrow after your sudden stop."

Dillon nodded and headed for the waiting arms of their grandmother. She may be hard as nails sometimes, but she knew when to just be Gram.

Logan strode over to Jenna. "Is he alright?"

She looked up at him with watery eyes. "Yes, he is. I checked him all over. He's just shaken from his near miss. He must have fallen asleep out here. I should have looked for him after dinner. I didn't even give him anything to eat yet."

He crouched down next to her. "If he was really hungry, he would have barked. Don't blame yourself. This is Dillon's fault, not yours."

"It's just that—I was going to—I mean I posted—Darn it. I was trying to give him away. But now I know I can't. He's already grown on me." Her voice was filled with hurt, as if her own heart betrayed her by loving Butterball.

He grinned. "Of course, you did. Who could resist that face?" He opened his palm toward the dog's pushed-in, long-jowled face and stifled a laugh.

Luckily, his ploy worked, and Jenna smiled. "I see your point." She gave Butterball a hug then stood. "How am I going to get home now? I have Whisper's truck at my house, but I need to call this in to my insurance company. From the look of it, there's no way I can get my insurance card out of my glove compartment."

He opened his mouth to invite her to stay, but had the sinking feeling that Dillon wouldn't be leaving before morning and he couldn't go to his brother's since Lacey and Cole already had guests. As much as Logan wanted it, he couldn't suggest it. "I can take you two home."

"Thank you." She bent over and patted Butterball again, as if reassuring herself he was still alive. "I'll see if my bag of tricks is still in one piece. That would not only be expensive to replace, but would take a couple days."

He followed her to the car but kept her away from it. If anything shifted, he didn't want it to shift on her. Opening the back door on the driver's side carefully, he pulled out her bag.

Butterball tried to get in, proving he was more than ready to go home. Luckily, Jenna held him back.

"Is that it?"

"No, my purse was on the front seat."

He opened the driver side door. With only the porch light from the house, he couldn't see much, so he felt round with his hand. He stepped away and closed the door. "I'm afraid that's not coming out tonight.

"Great. If I drive without a license and get stopped, I'll be fined."

"Tell you what. I'll come get you tomorrow and bring you where you need to go."

Her eyes widened, then turned mischievous. "I thought you had a cattle drive or something."

He chuckled. "Anything that needs to get done in the morning, Trace and Dillon can handle. I'm one-handed lately, so not as much help anyway."

She looked at her car one more time and sighed. "Okay. Let's go."

He escorted her to his truck and quickly had her and Butterball loaded in. As he sat in the driver's seat, he couldn't help but think how much more he would enjoy this ride with his present companion compared to the ride into the city earlier with Kylie. He held out little hope that she wasn't Charlotte's mom, but he had to be sure. Besides, it stalled the inevitable—sharing Charlotte.

As he drove them down the dirt road toward the Carefree Highway, he glanced at Jenna, who was deep in thought. He hadn't minded sharing his time with Charlotte tonight with her. In fact, when she looped her arm around his waist and kissed his child, it had felt so right that it caught him off guard.

Last year when Charlotte first came into his life, he bemoaned the fact that he was a single dad, but when Kylie showed up, he was ready to fight tooth and nail to keep it that way. So why was having Jenna with him and Charlotte suddenly so palatable?

"Take a left here. It's a dirt road."

That was no surprise. Any farm or ranch in the desert had a dirt road out to it. Only the small developments off the highway and the roads in the center of town were paved. It was still the wild west out here.

He turned onto the road and flicked on his high beams. Like Last Chance, there was nothing in the way of neighbors.

After a couple miles, the road simply ended in front of an old log farmhouse and barn. Both were weathered with age, even a couple shutters hanging by a single hinge, but the place looked like an old west homestead. "Wow."

Jenna squirmed in the seat next to him as he pulled to a stop. "I know. I just don't have the mo—time to fix the place up. It would take hiring the right people and being here while they worked and with my practice, it's just not a priority."

He'd be a complete idiot if he didn't recognize the defensiveness in her voice, but he prided himself on his intelligence. "This place is great. You're lucky."

Her hand on the door handle stilled. "Lucky?"

"Yes. You have this all to yourself out here. Sure it needs a little work, but talk about room to spread out. It's like living in a piece of history."

She studied him, probably trying to judge if he was joking.

"Just looking at this place in my headlights gives me an itch to get to work. Would you mind if I came out here during the day later this week to look around?"

Jenna's mouth opened then shut again. Finally, she simply nodded.

He smiled then jumped out of the truck and opened her door. She stepped out before turning to grab her bag. He took it from her and opened his arm toward the house. It really was a great structure. The single-story log home was unusual this far south. He'd only seen these in Prescott and farther north. At first glance, it looked relatively small, but he could see it stretched back toward a dark hill.

Jenna ducked under his arm and opened the back door of his cab. Butterball sat up and wagged his tail at her. She picked up the short-legged beast and put him on the ground. "He's heavier than he looks." Her new dog trotted forward and led them along a path lined with rocks to the front porch. "Watch the second step. It's broken on the left."

He skipped the step all together. If he broke it more, she would be mortified. "How did you find this place?"

She stopped to look back at him. "I didn't. My parents did. This is where I grew up. I bought it from my dad so he could move to Sedona."

Now his itch to return in the daylight doubled. He wanted to explore this place, to imagine Jenna playing in the yard. Did she wear pigtails?

"Oh, fudge. My keys are in my purse." She turned to look at him. "And no, I don't have a key hidden outside here. I thought about that, but then Javelinas came by and dug up the yard so I never got around to it."

He could understand having a problem with the wild pigs of the desert. "How about a window?"

She didn't look hopeful. "Living alone, I'm pretty good at locking up tight at night, but it's worth a shot."

By the light of his phone, they walked around the house, looking for an unlocked window. When they came to the back, Logan squinted into the darkness. "Is this a courtyard?"

Jenna stepped over the start of a wall about two logs high. "It was supposed to be, but my dad never finished it. It's been like this for over twenty years."

Excitement built in him. The potential of the place called to him and he had to tamp it back down. This wasn't his place.

"I think I found one." At Jenna's voice, he strode forward onto another porch.

She pointed toward the latch on the window with his phone. "Is that unlocked. I'm too short to be sure."

He looked at the latch in the light and grinned. "It is. Now we just need to get the screen out. What room is this in?"

"It's the kitchen. I like to open the window when I wash the dishes." She turned and gave Butterball a look. "I have a few more dishes to wash with him around, but I'm really glad he's here. I hope your cousin will be okay."

He shrugged. "He's tough, like the rest of us. Now let's see if we can get this screen off." Putting down her medical bag, he pushed his sling out of the way, and used his left hand on one side, while he bowed the aluminum to release the latch. The screen popped outward. After some twisting and turning, he pulled it off and opened the window with his good arm. He studied the small window frame. "Can you fit through that? I know I can't."

She sized up the window. "I think I can. You're hurt anyway. I wouldn't expect you to climb in there even if it was big enough." She walked up to the window. "I'm going to need a boost."

He started to bend over to cup his hands when his ribs reminded him to return his arm to his sling. Without a second thought, he got down on one knee. "Step right here."

"Are you sure?"

"Trust me." Though he said it off-handedly, he could see she took it a lot deeper, which had him anxious to meet her expectations. "I won't let you down. I promise."

Jenna didn't say anything. Instead, she put her foot on his thigh and hoisted herself up and through the window. As soon she was through, Butterball rose on his hind legs and put his paw on Logan's thigh. He chuckled. "No boy, we're going around to the front door."

Jenna spoke from inside. "Hold on. I'll open the back door and turn on a light."

He coaxed the dog down and rose. Picking up her veterinarian bag, he turned to face the darkened courtyard. Light flooded the area.

Damn. The log home was shaped like a U without the last wall being finished. The entire inside of it was porch with an empty area in the middle. What a great place for kids to grow up. He could almost imagine Jenna and her sister playing there.

"Thank you for bringing me home." Her voice from the door indicated it was time to leave.

Logan walked toward her and she ushered him inside. The warm wood of the rounded logs made it homey, even if he was only in an entryway. Across from him was the front door.

He set her bag down and closed the door after Butterball waddled in. "I'll pick you up tomorrow. What time do you need to be at work?"

She looked so uncomfortable with him being there. Where was his confident Dr. Jenna? Was she really that ashamed of such a unique home?

"My first appointment is at eight, but you don't have to do that. I'll drive Whisper's truck in. If I go the speed limit, there should be no reason for me to be stopped. Maybe you could call me when I can get my purse?" She had her arms crossed over her chest and didn't quite look him in the eye.

He stepped closer. "I can do better than that. I'll deliver your purse to you." He tipped her head up to look at him. "It will give me an excuse to see you tomorrow."

Her eyes widened. "You need an excuse?"

He smirked. "I don't, but in case you were thinking of avoiding me, I want a legit reason in your mind to see you."

She relaxed at that, and her hands came up to rest on his shoulders. "Thank you. I'd like that."

Logan lowered his head and gave her a goodnight kiss. He meant it to be short, but the second he tasted her, he couldn't resist and with his good arm, pulled her against him, wanting more than ever to make love to her again. If only he could stay.

A loud fart spoiled the moment and he pulled away as a strong smell followed.

"Butterball, really?" Jenna stepped away from the dog and him. "I'm sorry. He does that once in a while. I need to figure out what food is making him gassy."

He laughed as he waved the air in front of him and stepped to the front door. "I'll see you tomorrow."

Leaving the house quickly, he strode to his truck, a new excitement building inside. He had no idea why or what it was about, but it felt good. For the first time in a long time, he dared to hope his luck was changing.

When he arrived home, he found his Gram waiting in the kitchen for him. Since she was usually in bed watching television by now, he immediately went to the fridge and pulled out a beer. "Is Dillon alright?" He unscrewed the cap and threw it in the trash, then leaned his ass against the counter.

"He'll be sore tomorrow. He called his insurance company and they're sending someone out. He said he almost hit Dr. Jenna's dog."

He took a swallow of beer, not sure he wanted to comment on that.

"Dillon will be staying upstairs in the other bedroom that actually has a bed. Your grandfather left the other one inhabitable. Still, you'll need to make some room in the bathroom for him."

Great. Looked like his time alone upstairs was over. "I will. What happened?"

Gram sighed, her brow lowered in confusion. "Your Aunt Beverly has gone too far this time. I'm not sure if she'll ever get her boys back now."

His Aunt had been determined to marry off one of her boys to a wealthy, well-known Arizona family since they were toddlers. Now that they were men, her efforts had quadrupled.

It was one of the reasons Cole had joined his grandparents on Last Chance.

Now it looked like she'd alienated Dillon, too. "I'm glad our mom has been so much more reasonable. She can't even complain that she doesn't have grandchildren yet. I should take Charlotte down there next weekend." He took another swallow.

His grandmother fixed him with that look that he dreaded. Dammit, what did he do now?

Gram pointed to the seat across from her. "We need to talk, Logan."

Hell, he didn't like the sound of this. Bringing his beer with him, he took the seat she indicated. "What do we need to talk about?"

"Dr. Jenna to start." She fixed him with a serious stare that made him want to fidget in his chair.

"Okay."

"What are you doing? Is this a serious thing or do you plan to sleep with her and move on because I'll tell you right now, I don't approve of that." Though his grandmother had taken down her hair to get ready for bed, it didn't soften her features at all as she zeroed in on her point.

"It's not like that. I like Jenna. We are just taking it one day at a time. It suits *both* of us." Even though his gut said Jenna would like something more concrete, she'd agreed, so he'd go with that.

"She's a good, hard-working woman and deserves the same in a man." He opened his mouth to argue, but she gave him the raised eyebrow and he closed his mouth. "I'll give you the hard-working, but your morals are questionable. Either you make up your mind about Dr. Jenna or you let her go. She doesn't need someone messing up her life after all she's done to be successful despite her—her childhood."

129

Jenna's childhood wasn't all roses? That was the first he'd heard of that. "What do you mean, Gram?"

"It's not my place to tell tales out of school. Maybe she hasn't told you because she doesn't trust you. That's a sign."

He didn't like the punch to the gut his grandmother's statement threw at him. Jenna didn't trust him. Hell. He took a gulp of beer.

"Now when are these DNA results supposed to come back?"

Putting his beer bottle back on the table, he glanced at the calendar hanging on the refrigerator. "The day after tomorrow. I paid for expedited delivery. They'll come here. I think I can go online as well, but they don't make that available until the day after."

"Then you have a couple days to decide how you want to handle Kylie in your life. Something Dr. Jenna will want to know, I'm sure."

"Whoa, I don't know yet that Kylie will need to be in my life. That's the whole point of the DNA test."

His grandmother looked at him like he was an idiot. "Logan, what possible reason would a stranger have for finding where you live to be a mother to your daughter?"

He looked away. Absolutely none, unless she was some psycho who lost her baby and wanted to be a mother to his. He shook his head to dispel that particular movie plot from his brain. "Right, but I don't want her in Charlotte's life. She has a criminal past and even now she's working at a fast food restaurant and can't write past the fourth-grade level."

Gram's eyebrows rose. "That doesn't mean she won't be a wonderful mother to Charlotte."

"But I don't want to share her." The words were out of his mouth before he could take them back. It sounded like he was a little kid who didn't want to share his toys, but it was far more than that. "I want Charlotte to have a perfect life."

For the first time in months, his grandmother's eyes softened while looking at him. She reached across the table and patted his hand. "I know you do, but life isn't perfect." She pulled her hand back. "I think you should consider having Kylie move closer. I'd say take the extra bedroom upstairs, but Dillon will be staying for a while."

Every muscle in his body screamed against that suggestion and he rose. "No. I won't have her under the same roof."

"You don't have to, but you need to come to terms with the fact that Charlotte deserves to know her mother. There is a bond between a child and a parent, you know that, and a mother and daughter's bond can be very strong. Why do you think the courts give custody to the mother a majority of the time?"

Fear of losing his daughter sliced through his heart. "No. That's why I have a lawyer. I won't give up custody of Charlotte. What's wrong with you? I thought you loved Charlotte. If you can't handle taking care of her while I'm working, I'll find someone who can."

Gram's eyes turned calculating. "You mean like Dr. Jenna? Or do you mean Kylie?"

He grabbed up his beer bottle and strode out of the kitchen.

"Logan Williams come back here!"

He ignored his grandmother's command and stormed out onto the porch and down the steps. He couldn't believe what she suggested. Give Charlotte into the care of Kylie? The woman who dropped her child off on his doorstep in the middle of a winter night?

Gram's betrayal hit him hard, and he swallowed the rest of his beer in one chug. He didn't care what anyone thought. He would never allow Kylie to have Charlotte.

~~*~~

Jenna unlocked her front door and rushed in. "Come on Butterball, we don't have much time." Since the dog was in no hurry, she left the door open and dropped her medical bag on the bench below the three coat hooks on the wall. The hooks were rarely used except during the dead of winter when she needed a light jacket, but when she and her sister were little, the hooks were used for their book bags.

Rushing into the kitchen, she washed her hands before pulling out a large pot and filling it with water. Setting it on the 19th century wood stove replica that actually heated with gas, she turned it on high.

She stepped to the cabinets and took out a box of penne pasta. Moving to the ice box replica refrigerator, she hoped her homemade sauce was completely defrosted. She opened the door and pulled it out, along with a bottle of wine. In the limited time she'd spent with Logan, she's only seen him drink beer and water. Did he even like wine?

"Fine time to be thinking about that, right, BB?" She raised her brows at him as he lumbered into the kitchen. She walked to the entry to close the door, but hesitated. The sky was spitting a pretty pink glow across her valley, the sunset barely beginning as the sun passed behind the hill at the back of her house.

Finally, she shut the door and returned to the kitchen. Taking out another pot, she poured her sauce into it, the sound of a hard chunk hitting the bottom made her groan. She glanced at the clock. Logan was due in less than thirty minutes.

Darn it. She still needed to tidy up, feed the dog and shower. There was no way she'd be ready in time. She looked at Butterball. "You want your dinner, too, don't you?"

He lifted his head up at her and appeared to smile. She

grinned in return. It was just impossible not to when he did that. "Logan will just have to wait for dinner, but you will get yours now."

She pulled Butterball's food out from the lower cabinet. She wasn't going to panic because she was late. Mrs. Thompson's kitty's surgery had been more complicated than expected. Connie had volunteered to stay to watch over the elderly cat, which had been a blessing or Jenna would have had to cancel dinner.

Once Butterball was happy, she turned off the stove and headed down the hall to her bedroom. It still looked masculine from when her father had it, but she liked it. She hadn't done any redecorating since he'd sold her the house. It just wasn't a priority. What would Logan think about it?

Taking off her clothes, she threw them in the wash and took a step toward the bathroom when her phone rang. She didn't have time to talk, but if it was Connie, she had to answer.

Picking up her phone, she recognized the number. "Hello, Logan."

"Hi, I'm not going to make it tonight. I'm sorry." His voice sounded too polite. Not like him.

"Is everything okay?"

A couple of seconds of silence gave her the answer. Did it have to do with why he didn't drop off her purse at the office and sent Whisper by with it instead?

"Yes, it's fine. I just have no one here to watch Charlotte. Gram had to run up to Prescott this afternoon and she isn't back yet. Dillon is here, but…"

But he didn't trust his cousin with his daughter. "Do you want to bring her over with you?"

"No." The reply was quick and definite. As if he realized that, he continued. "I don't want to keep her up past her bedtime."

"I understand." She did. What she didn't understand is the new tone of his voice. "We can do it another time."

"Thanks for understanding. Bye."

Huh? No, "I'll call you tomorrow" or "How about this weekend"? Just "bye"? She sat on her bed, staring at the phone as if it could tell her what went on in Logan's head. The man would drive her crazy if she kept her focus on him. Setting her phone back on the bed, she stepped into the shower.

As she dried off, her phone rang again. Did Annette come home in time after all? Grabbing up the phone, she answered. "Hello?"

"Sorry Jenna, but I think you need to come here. Snowy isn't doing so well."

Fudge. "Okay, I'm on my way."

Hanging up, she quickly dressed and headed to the kitchen. Butterball, having finished his dinner, sat at the door to go outside.

"Well BB, it looks like we're going back to work." She opened the door to let him do his business, then walked into the kitchen. Throwing the pot of sauce into the fridge, she hoped Connie would pick up dinner for her.

Grabbing up her bag, she walked out, locked the door and headed for Whisper's truck. She was lucky Whisper didn't mind her using it until she could get the insurance money. She really should buy her own truck, but she doubted she could swing the payments with only her car's value for a down payment. She'd be better off buying a used car and having no payments.

"Come, Butterball." She slapped her hand against her thigh. Her inherited dog waddled toward her as fast as he could go, his tongue lolling out the side of his mouth. "I'll get you some more water at the office."

As if he understood, Butterball lapped his lips, closed his

mouth and sat on the ground in front of the truck. It was far too high for him to jump, so she lifted him into the cab and hopped in after him. She'd hoped it would be a long night...but not this way.

Chapter Ten

"**D**ammit Trace, will you hold it still?" Logan scowled at his brother.

"If you think you can do better, then you hold it and let me pound that in."

"Right." He handed over the mallet, more than happy to give his sore ribs a break. By bracing his left hip against the workbench, he was able to hold the broken harness in place for Trace to complete the repair.

"Let's test it. If it holds, we can deliver the new one to Sanders before dinner." Trace hauled the harness off the table and they walked out to where Cyclone was tied to the corral. Except Cyclone wasn't there.

"Damn horse." Logan stared at another broken fence rail.

Trace pointed. "That's going to be a problem when Tiny Dancer goes into heat next year."

Logan looked to the south corral where they left Tiny Dancer. Cyclone was standing just outside the fence facing the petite, crooked-legged horse. Macy and the colt were in their shelter. "We'll have to stable her at Cole's. Cyclone won't be happy about that either."

"I know."

He followed his brother to the Clydesdale. As soon as they

set the harness on the horse's back, he gave them his attention. Buckling it on, Trace walked Cyclone to the pile of lumber at the back of the barn where it was dumped by the delivery truck earlier that morning.

While his brother loaded the old wagon, he attached the harness to it. "That's enough. The more trips Cyclone has to make, the better." He handed the reins to Trace.

"Thanks." His brother flicked them and Cyclone started walking.

Logan watched the two head down the dirt road toward Cole's house. His cousin was in for a surprise if Trace made it all the way there. He had no idea the lumber for his small stable had arrived.

Logan turned away and strode into the barn to put away the tools. Trace had been the only one he'd spoken to except his daughter today. Gram stayed overnight in Prescott, which was just as well. It pissed him off that her betrayal hurt so much, but he still wouldn't budge on his stance about Kylie. Neither would she.

She could rule her own home, but he would have the final say in his daughter's life. That was his decision to make and his alone. But she'd been right about one thing. He had to decide what he would allow.

After a long talk with his lawyer, which he was sure cost him a month's salary, he'd decided to agree to supervised visitation if he had to. If she asked for anything more, he'd fight her. His lawyer said the more he would allow, the easier it would be to convince the court, but that was as far as he would go.

He still couldn't believe a court would take Charlotte from him and hand her over to a woman who abandoned her and admittedly had worked on the wrong side of the law. Unfortunately, his lawyer didn't think those issues would be difficult for her to sway to her side because as he said, the courts were partial to the mother—child bond.

Screw that. He slammed the mallet into the cabinet and the shelf shook. Two loose shoeing nails fell onto the barn floor. Damn. Crouching down, he picked them up and returned them to the shelf. His ribs were as much a pain as his Gram's words right now. The old woman had really burrowed under his skin and sent his mind in a hundred directions. Unfortunately, one of those directions was about Jenna.

Closing the cabinet, he ground his teeth. Gram's attitude about him and Jenna had been pretty clear. Jenna deserved the best and if he wanted her, he needed to step up to the starting gate. That scared the bull crap out of him. A day at a time he could handle.

But Gram was right. What if after months of days at a time Jenna's feelings changed? What if getting to know him made her not want him anymore? The last person he'd had a close relationship with was his dad and that had blown up in his face. Not only had his dad become incapacitated, but he'd lost who he was.

Logan cracked his knuckles one by one and leaned against a stall. He'd never admit it to anyone, but the man he'd admired and loved with soul-seared adulation, had turned mean, selfish, and nasty. He didn't like the man his father became after the first stroke and the second made it worse. It was like his father was a stranger.

He'd put his dad on a pedestal and then…his heart constricted at the remembered pain. The fact was, he lost his father long before his dad died and that had colored his memory and their relationship. He hadn't wanted to get that close to another person again and then his daughter arrived. She would change and grow into her own person forcing him to risk his heart with her. Did he dare risk it with Jenna, too?

Pushing away from the wall, Logan strode out of the barn. He didn't want to think about any of it anymore. He needed to get some work done and keep his mind on easy tasks, not soul searching. Heading for the south corral and the new colt, he stopped at the sound of a vehicle.

Turning, he recognized Whisper's truck. Damn, it had to be Jenna. He hadn't called her since he bailed on their date. Did Cole call her? With little choice, he strode toward the truck.

She hopped out and came around the front, no bag in her hand. "Hi." Her smile was friendly, so she must have forgiven him. She opened the passenger door and lifted Butterball down. "Now don't cause any trouble this time."

As Butterball trotted off, his significant backside swinging side to side, Logan greeted Jenna with a smile of his own. His mind was still conflicted but his heart was happy to see her. She walked right up to him, and he couldn't resist pulling her into his arms and giving her a thorough kiss.

When he finally released her, her cheeks were flushed.

"Wow, I didn't realize I was so missed."

He grinned. "You were."

She held her arms around his waist loosely, her head tipped back to meet his gaze. "I missed you too, though it turned out that had you made it to dinner last night, I would have had to bail myself."

Relief helped him relax. "Why?"

"I had a tough surgery yesterday and last night it was touch and go. Luckily, by this morning, the kitty was already meowing for food, so it looks like a full recovery is eminent."

He let her go and stepped back. "Then I'm glad it all worked out for the best. Did Cole call you? He didn't say anything to me."

She cocked her head and put a hand on her hip. "No, Cole

didn't call me. I'm not here on ranch business. I'm here to see you."

Since she'd never come to the ranch except for the horses, it surprised him. "Me? But you work in the afternoon." Now he sounded dumb. *Get your act together.*

"I work all day, usually. What I don't usually do is work all night. I had Connie reschedule most of my afternoon so I could leave early and go home for some sleep. I just thought I'd stop over here first and see how you were."

"Why would you need to check on me? In case you haven't noticed, I'm not a horse." He winked. "Then again, I have been compared to one on occasion."

Jenna rolled her eyes. "Oh please, I've seen what you have. Remember?"

Their evening in the hay came to mind and his body responded. "Hmm, I don't think I do. Maybe I need to show you again."

She laughed. It wasn't a dainty giggle. Jenna had a full sounding laugh that made him want to hold her tight and never let her go. Maybe that was exactly what he needed to do. To hell with the day to day thing. Maybe jumping in with both his feet was what he should do. It had worked with his baby girl.

"That sounds like fun, but how about after I get some rest. I'd be worthless right now. I just stopped by because last night when you called you sounded too polite. I figured something must be bothering you, besides your Gram not getting back in time."

He took her hand and headed for the porch. "You are very perceptive. Let me get you a drink."

"Okay. I'll have some ice tea."

He stopped in front of the two chairs to the left of the door. "You relax. I'll be right back."

He strode inside and poured two glasses of tea. What was he thinking? One minute he didn't want to be close to Jenna and then she shows up and he's all in. He needed to have his head examined. Or maybe Jenna was a good influence on him. Definitely something to think about.

Picking up the glasses, he brought them out to the porch and handed her one. Moving the other chair right next to hers, he waited for her to take a sip. "Tell me about this complicated surgery you had."

She set her glass down and shook her head. "First, you tell me what was bothering you last night."

"That? That was just me disagreeing with Gram the night before. It put me in a bad mood. That's a daily occurrence around here."

She reached over and took his hand in hers. "What did you argue about?"

"Who said we argued?" At her look, he gave in. He really didn't want to talk about it. "We just disagreed about Kylie."

She stilled. "You mean your grandmother wanted you to marry her and you refused?"

He chuckled. "Damn, right I'd refuse. But that wasn't Gram's issue. In fact, she thinks you are quite a catch."

"Really?" Jenna's genuine surprise was refreshing.

"Yes, really." He cupped his hand behind her neck and gave her another kiss. When they separated, he continued to hold her there so he could be sure she listened. "I don't remember her exact words but it was something about how smart and beautiful you are."

She pulled out of his grasp. "Now I know you're just laying on the charm. Your grandmother might approve of my independence, but looks would never come into it."

"You're right. Guess it was just how I remembered it."

"So was that what bothered you? That your Gram liked me?"

He chuckled at that. "Damn, but you're like a dog with a bone."

"Funny, my dad says that about me." She lifted her glass in salute.

"He's right."

She finished swallowing and stared at him. Her teal green eyes were fascinating. Sometimes the blue was stronger but other times, like now, the green was stronger. Could it be a reflection of her emotions?

"Logan, you're stalling."

He blinked. "No, I was just distracted by you." She opened her mouth and he spoke before she could say anything. "Gram wanted me to let Kylie in Charlotte's life. She said Charlotte deserves to know her mother, but you met her. She's not mother material."

Jenna's expression turned serious. "That may be, but your Gram is right. Charlotte does deserve to know her mother, flaws and all."

His gut tightened at the same time his heart skipped a beat. Not her, too? Was it some kind of secret woman thing? "I don't agree. Charlotte doesn't need Kylie's influence in her life. There are plenty of good role models for her right here on the farm." *And I thought you could be one of them. Don't prove me wrong.*

"And that's why it's important for Charlotte to know her mom. Without that, there will always be a void in her life, no matter how many women fuss over her. No one is perfect. Even Charlotte is going to disappoint you one day."

"She won't. She can't. She's my daughter."

Jenna leaned forward, her look intense. "And Kylie is her mother. That is a special bond that shouldn't be severed."

It was too much. Logan stood. "Kylie broke that bond when she left my daughter on the porch of my home in the middle of the night. That she comes back over a year later wanting to be a part of Charlotte's life again doesn't mean a thing. There's a good chance she'll just up and disappear again and then what do I tell Charlotte while she's crying from a broken heart, thinking her mother has abandoned her and doesn't love her any more? And then what happens if Kylie returns again?"

Jenna rose as well, her gaze sympathetic but determined. "Then Charlotte will be thrilled her mom is back and if she leaves again she'll have you to turn to. You can't protect her from that. You don't have the right to keep them apart. You have to let Charlotte know her mother."

"No, I don't. I won't let anyone hurt her. Not even her own mother."

"That's not your decision to make."

He fisted his hands to keep from lashing out. He wanted to knock over the furniture, break a window, anything to stop the hurt of betrayal from eating away at his heart. He hadn't expected it from her, which made it harder to take. "It *is* my decision to make and I have made it. Now I think you should leave."

Jenna's eyes widened in surprise. "That's how you will settle this? By asking me to leave?"

"If you can't support me, then we have nothing further to talk about."

"It's not that I—okay." She turned to the steps and jogged down them. "Butterball! Butterball, come." She patted her leg as she walked toward her truck.

Part of him wanted to grab her and keep her from leaving, but his heart hurt too much to act on that. If she was going to be in his life, she'd have to support his decisions regarding

Charlotte. If she couldn't do that, it was better he found out now before they grew too close.

Butterball waddled to her and she picked him up, hugging him before setting him on the seat. Maybe that was it. Maybe Jenna was so attuned to animals that she couldn't see what it was like to be a parent to a child.

To be fair, he hadn't known either until Charlotte arrived on his doorstep, but whoever shared his life would need to understand the bond he had with his daughter. A bond that was more precious than anything, even his own happiness.

As Jenna backed up the truck and headed down the dirt road, he tried to ignore the burning sensation in his chest, but he knew what it was. He was watching his chance at happiness drive away.

~~*~~

Logan held his daughter in his good arm as he stood outside the south corral fence. Today was his last day to have her all to himself. The DNA results would arrive and he wouldn't be able to keep Kylie away any longer. His luck had run true to form.

"Horzie!" Charlotte squealed, pointing with cowboy teddy in hand at the colt as he jumped out of the shelter, shaking his head with his sudden starts and stops. "Horzie!" She pounded the teddy on his chest. "Da-da. Horzie."

He smiled at her excitement despite his mood. "That's right. It's a horsey and it's Charlotte's horsey."

She turned away from the corral and looked at him with wide eyes. "Horzie mine?"

Her awe was rewarding and humbling, making his eyes misty at the thought he would have to share these kinds of moments in the future. He kept his voice soft. "Yes. The horzie is Charlotte's."

Her green eyes sparkled with glee before she let rip an ear-piercing squeal.

He hugged her to him despite her squirming then loosened his hold. She held out both her hands toward the colt who now stood transfixed after her yell. "Horzie, mine. Want mine horzie." She leaned precariously out over his arm and he grasped her torso to keep her from falling, wincing at the pull on his left side.

"Whoa, there. You don't want to scare it. Shh." Her eyes moved down, then to the right before she looked directly at him with that unseeing stare that told him her little mind was processing the information. She would be one smart young lady someday.

Finally, she pressed one of her chubby fingers to her lips and blew.

He barely contained his laugh. "Yes, we need to be quiet."

She blew against her finger then turned with it still pressed to her mouth to look at the colt who was back to romping around.

Logan stepped closer to the fence and clicked his tongue.

The baby horse stopped and looked up.

Charlotte remained completely still.

He clicked his tongue again and the colt walked over. He held out his hand and the colt lowered his head and licked at his palm.

Charlotte remained transfixed.

He kept his voice to a whisper to signal her to be quiet. "Do you want to touch your horsey?"

She didn't answer. Instead, she leaned over his arm forcing him to pull his hand away from the colt to catch her before she tumbled into the corral. The movement hurt, but it was nothing to what he'd feel if she fell.

The colt raised its head at the same time Charlotte reached

out and her hand brushed its coat. As she waved her hand up and down at the surprise contact, squealing with delight, the colt bounded away.

Logan stifled a chuckle, not wanting his ribs to hurt anymore then they already did from his daughter's antics. He readjusted her, settling her back onto his good arm. "Wait until daddy teaches you to ride. Then you will be really happy."

Charlotte started to push up and down. "Ride horzie."

He turned back toward the house. "Yes, you will get to ride your horsey, but first you will need to name it. Not everyone is happy with Charlotte's Horse as a name."

Charlotte didn't pay any attention. She'd twisted around and watched her horse from over his shoulder.

He walked into the unusually quiet house. Gram was still in Prescott with her sick friend and Trace hadn't arrive yet.

Since he was almost worthless in helping around the ranch, he planned to spend the whole day with Charlotte.

He brought her into the kitchen and settled her into her highchair. He should probably wake up Dillon, but he was enjoying his time alone with Charlotte too much. Grabbing her dry oat cereal, he dropped a handful onto her tray. She immediately put pieces in her mouth, and he surreptitiously pulled the teddy from the tray and set it on the shelf behind her.

Scrambled eggs with cheese was one of her favorite meals, so he took out a bowl and started cracking eggs.

"More, da-da." Charlotte banged her tray with her hands.

He looked over his shoulder to find her tray empty. Wiping his hands, he poured out more cereal then went back to preparing the eggs. Rifling through the fridge, he found bacon and leftover potatoes from dinner the night before. Pulling them out along with half of a large onion, he started on hash browns.

A piece of cereal pinged the stove where he cooked, and he turned.

Charlotte laughed. "More, da-da."

He stepped to his left to grab the cereal and his boot crunched beneath him. "What?" Looking down, he found cereal all over the floor. "Charlotte, you don't throw your food."

His perfect daughter hit him in the face with another cereal piece. He scowled. "No."

A pop from the bacon forced him to turn back to the food he cooked. He waited until everything was done then he turned off the burners under the pans and wiped his hands on a towel. Moving to his daughter's tray, which still held a few cereal missiles, he scooped them up and threw them in the trash.

"Bad da-da. More."

"No, no more. Your food is not a toy." He moved to the closet and pulled the broom out, sweeping up the cereal and disposing of it.

"Da-da more! More! More!"

He pulled a chair up to her and gave her his full attention. "Charlotte was a bad girl." He kept his tone even and calm.

She looked at him and shook her head. "No. Da-da bad. More."

"Charlotte, food is for eating not throwing." He frowned at her, wanting her to understand this was an important lesson.

She stared at him and her bottom lip started to quiver.

Ah hell. He wanted to lift her up and hug her, but she'd never learn that way. "If I give you more, will you eat?" He took a fork from the table and motioned with it.

Her lip stopped and she gave him that far off stare as her mind worked. "Eat."

He smiled. "Good girl."

Getting up, he put a small amount of the eggs on her baby plate and blew on it to cool it off.

"Eat. Eat. Eat. Eat." She was back to banging on her tray.

He set a plate of food at his seat then brought her dish. Sitting next to her, he scooped eggs into his mouth. "Hmmm, good."

She watched him then picked up her eggs with her hand and stuffed them in her mouth. "Hmmm."

He almost choked on his laugh, but quickly squelched it for both his rib's sake and his daughter's sake.

"What smells so good?" Dillon strode into the kitchen, his short black hair sticking up, his gray sweat pants hanging below his waist and no shirt.

"It's breakfast, but you're not getting any until you put on a shirt."

His cousin stopped, his hand on the cabinet handle. "What do you mean, put on a shirt? I always eat breakfast in sweats."

Logan gave him a frown. "Not in this house. I have a young daughter growing up here. So if you want some of the breakfast I cooked, you put on a shirt. Might as well comb your hair while you're at it."

"Are you serious?"

"Completely."

"Okay, okay." Dropping his hand from the cabinet door, he turned around and headed down the hallway.

Logan grinned as he heard Dillon running up the stairs. His food must smell exceptionally good.

He returned his attention to Charlotte who promptly asked for more eggs. Checking the floor around her and seeing none there, he scooped another spoonful onto her plate and cooled them before giving them to her.

"Now, can I eat?" Dillon walked back into the room, a black

t-shirt with some rock band Logan never heard of plastered across the front.

Since the logo only had a name and a white convertible, he didn't find it objectionable. Though the convertible just reminded him of what would happen today. "Go ahead, but leave some for Trace. I'm sure he'll want to eat when he gets here."

"Got it." Dillon moved to the stove.

Having his cousin show up could actually benefit Last Chance since he was of so little use with his broken ribs at the moment. "You're timing is perfect. Trace and I talked it over and we need you to keep Cyclone busy."

Dillon piled his plate with eggs. "That's the Clydesdale, right? The one that needs special attention?"

"Yes. In addition to attention and finding things for him to hall, his feathered feet need to be cleaned of any mud."

His cousin nodded. "I can do that, though I doubt he'll be seeing much mud around here."

There was that. "I'd also appreciate it if you could take Black Jack out for a ride, that is if you don't have any long-term effects from your crash."

Dillon kept his eyes on the food, adding strips of bacon to his plate. "Just a couple sore muscles. Better if I move around anyway."

Logan tried to imagine what his Aunt Bev could have done to piss off the second of her two sons so much that he'd leave their horse ranch.

At New Year's, before Cole and Lacey's surprise wedding, his aunt was still trying to get Cole interested in a wealthy woman she'd brought to the party with her, even though she knew Cole was engaged. "So, what did your mother pull this time?"

Dillon sat down with a heaping plate of eggs, bacon and

hash browns. "Let's just say she went too far. When I refused to do what she wanted, she threatened to take the horses away. I told her to take her fucking ranch and shove it."

"Watch your mouth." He looked at his daughter who held her eggs in her hand.

"Luck. Luck."

He swallowed hard. "That's right. Daddy has terrible luck."

"Lucky da-da." She stuffed another handful of eggs into her mouth and grinned.

He smiled at her before turning back to Dillon to scowl.

"Sorry. I'm not used to having kids around. I've been hanging out with too many cowboys. I'll try to be careful."

His cousin *did* look apologetic. "You do that." He returned his attention to his own eggs, his mind racing. Would Kylie swear in front of their daughter? Would she even care? He liked having Gram in Charlotte's life because she was a good role model, but Kylie could undo everything Gram did.

For the second time, he wished it had been Jenna who gave birth to his daughter. If that were true, they wouldn't have fought over having Charlotte's mother in her life.

Then again, Jenna would have never left her child on his doorstep.

Chapter Eleven

Jenna pulled into the parking area behind her office and turned off Whisper's truck. The breech cow delivery had been touch and go and very messy. She smelled of blood and guts and her belly balked. She'd always known she'd have calls like today's, but she didn't know she'd be making them in such a frazzled state of mind.

Yesterday on her drive home, she'd become more and more angry at Logan. The man was a stubborn ass, refusing to see the other side of an issue. He was completely blinded by his fatherhood.

She knew what it was like growing up without a mom. Not being able to talk to anyone, especially a parent, about female things like her periods, sex, or even just what color dress would look good with her complexion. She'd avoided her prom to skirt all those topics.

But it was more than that. There was nothing like a mother's love. She remembered her mom giving her hugs, telling her stories before she went to bed, and brushing her hair. Those mother-daughter times were just as special as father-daughter times…at least until she was seven. Part of her wanted to argue on behalf of Charlotte, but the other half wanted to argue for herself and her right to have an opinion without being shut off and cast away.

Then she'd arrived home and crawled into bed. That's when her heart broke. He didn't say it, but it was obvious he was done with her, and she cried herself to sleep.

Now, she just wanted to curl up in a ball and forget the world existed, but that wasn't her lot in life. She had a job to do, and it was an emotionally rewarding one if not always financially so. The Last Chance was her financial lifeline and she refused to give it up because Logan couldn't see past his own nose.

As her anger resurfaced, her focus became sharper. "You ready to see, Connie?" She looked at Butterball, who wagged his tail every time she spoke. "Or do you want to bite Logan's leg with your sharp teeth?"

Butterball wagged his tail again.

She grinned. Mr. Erickson must have known what he was doing when he gave her the dog. Just having Butterball around in her lonely, hectic life was a huge help to her psyche. "Okay, let's go see how the rest of the menagerie is doing."

Jumping out, she walked around to the passenger door and lifted Butterball down then grabbed her bag from the floor of the front seat. She walked to the back entrance and easily slipped into her office without anyone seeing her.

Pulling a dog bone from her desk draw, she held it out to Butterball. "That's for being such a good listener." He took the bone and waddled over to his bed, a present from Connie.

She flicked on her computer then used her bathroom to wash up with warm soapy water. The hose at the ranch had such hot water from the Arizona heat, that she'd barely been able to let it touch her skin.

When she returned to her desk, she sorted through her mail, setting aside the bills for the office and her student loans. "Oh, boy. I bet this is the insurance company's value for my car."

Butterball ignored her, having way too much fun with his

bone to bother with her. Even his tail didn't wag. Was that a sign?

Slicing open the envelope, she stared and her heart sank—$3,984.32. She'd never find a reliable used car for that amount, but it would be a halfway decent deposit on a new car. The problem was, she had her heart set on a small pickup truck about the size of Whisper's.

Taking out a calculator, she crunched the numbers three-ways to Tuesday, but it was no use. She couldn't afford a truck. Defeated, she crumbled up the paper she'd scribbled on.

Maybe she could ask Whisper if she'd like to sell hers? It wasn't like the woman used her own vehicle that much, and now that Trace was living with her and had a truck, she just might consider selling. The more Jenna thought of the idea, the more she liked it. "See BB, there's still hope."

Butterball continued to ignore her, so she checked on her next appointment. Having a few minutes before it started, she strode into the back room where her most critical patients were recovering. Luckily, there were very few, just a hamster, a duck and Snowy, Mrs. Thompson's elderly cat.

She checked each out and was pleased with their progress. The hamster could go home, but the duck needed another day and she'd watch Snowy for a few more days. Once satisfied they were all well, she stepped out into the waiting area. Connie handed her a file and she greeted Ms. Landry and the box of kittens she held.

Luckily, her appointments for the rest of the day kept her mind on her job. It wasn't until her last appointment left and she sat down in her office that her own heartache hit her all over again.

She tried to ignore it, typing in her final notes, but it was no use. She loved Logan Williams and he'd pushed her away again.

This time, there was no excuse except his stubbornness, and she refused to have her heart broken over that. She would just have to change his mind or they could agree to disagree because other than his refusal to see her side, he was a good man.

Feeling a lot better now that she'd made her decision, she closed down her computer.

"Excuse me, Dr. Jenna, but Mrs. Thompson is here. She'd like to talk to you." Connie looked puzzled, her eyebrows drawn down in confusion. "She saw the closed sign but knocked anyway. I was rather put out, but since her kitty is here, I had to let her in."

"Of course you did. That was the right thing to do." She studied her receptionist. "Did you call her to update her on Snowy's progress?"

"I did. Every morning and evening. I even called her while you were in with your last patient to tell her how well Snowy was doing this evening."

No wonder Connie was puzzled. "Bring her down here and you can go home. I'll lock up."

"Are you sure?"

She nodded. "Positive. I have a lot less to do tonight than you do."

Connie grinned. "I *do* have another dinner and dance planned with my cowboy and I need to change for that."

"Go ahead. I'm sure this won't take long."

Connie nodded before disappearing from the doorway and returning with Mrs. Thompson.

Jenna rose. "Hello, Mrs. Thompson. What can I help you with?"

The older woman grasped her large purse in both hands. "I miss Snowy so much. I was wondering if I could see her?"

Jenna's heart melted. "Is Snowy your only pet?"

The woman nodded.

Jenna glanced at Butterball, who was curled up and snoring. She now had a new appreciation for the bond between pet and pet owner. "Then let's go see her."

Mrs. Thompson's face relaxed, and she smiled gratefully.

Jenna led the way to the back room where only the duck and Snowy resided. She pointed to the cat cage where Snowy was sleeping.

Mrs. Thompson stepped close. "Snowy, your mommy's here."

The cat immediately opened its eyes and rose to a sitting position.

Mrs. Thompson had tears in her eyes. "Can I touch her?"

"Of course."

The older woman put her fingers through the cage bars and Snowy immediately rubbed her face against her. Jenna quietly stepped out of the room, letting the two companions have their time.

She walked back into her office and stared at Butterball, who was curled up on his bed, his pale, tan fur all that was visible which explained where he got his name. On one hand, she wanted to hug him to her, but she also didn't want to disturb his sleep.

Footsteps up the hall had her turning back toward her door. Mrs. Thompson was smiling, her whole demeanor completely changed. She placed her hand on Jenna's arm.

"Dr. Jenna, you don't know how much this meant to me."

"I'm happy I could help."

The woman's hand tightened. "No, I mean what you did for Snowy. Every vet in the city I took her to said she had lived a good life at sixteen and it was time to let her go. Others said it was too risky to operate on such an old cat, but they could prescribe medicine to keep her out of pain."

Jenna swallowed, glad she hadn't known that beforehand. Many of her clients had cats that lived into their early twenties, so she hadn't considered Snowy too old for surgery. Still, she was pretty sure the trauma of the operation would take a toll on the cat.

"Mrs. Thompson, you need to understand. I took out the tumor in her stomach, but that doesn't mean another one won't form. Also, it will take a lot for her to recover from this, and she will need to eat completely differently. I can't guarantee you will have much more time with her."

Mrs. Thompson removed her hand and delved into her purse. "I know all that. You have gone above and beyond a typical vet, and I want to show you my appreciation."

"Oh no, that's fine. You will get a bill when you take her home." Jenna grabbed the woman's hand as she lifted an envelope from her purse.

"It's just a card, honey."

Feeling a little foolish, she accepted it. "Thank you. It's nice to be appreciated."

Mrs. Thompson grinned. "I know it is. When can I bring Snowy home?"

Jenna kept her smile to herself because she knew Connie would have told the older woman. "Probably in a couple more days. I want to be sure Snowy can eat and drink normally before she leaves with you."

"Can I come by and see her tomorrow?"

She wanted to tell her she couldn't, but the look of hope in the woman's eyes made her give in. "Of course you can. Just schedule a time with Connie, okay?"

Mrs. Thompson nodded. "I will. Thank you again." The woman turned away and let herself out.

Jenna locked the door behind her and turned out the lights.

When she entered her office, Butterball was awake and wagging his tail again. Dropping the card on her desk, she grabbed her purse, leaving her medical bag there. She had no ranch calls to make in the morning. The only ranch call she had to make right now was to confront a certain stubborn cowboy.

"Ready BB?"

Her dog gave her that special smile of his and waddled out ahead of her. His actions gave her an idea. Maybe there was more than one way to melt a man's heart and change his mind at the same time.

❧ Logan tensed at the knock on the door as Charlotte played with her blocks on the family room rug. This was it. The moment of truth. The truth he didn't want to accept. Lifting Charlotte, cowboy teddy in one hand, two blocks in her other, he set her down in her playpen and stood too quickly, his ribs reminding him he wasn't a hundred percent yet.

Another knock sounded and he strode down the hall to the front door, sure the delivery person would hear his boots. When he opened the door, the man was just turning away.

"You have a delivery for me?" *That I don't want.*

The man turned back and had him sign, then handed him a simple letter size envelope.

He closed the door and stared at it. What was he afraid of? He'd already accepted the worst case as the inevitable, but while he didn't know for sure, there was that niggling bit of hope still out there.

Who was he kidding? He had the worst luck. Of all the one night stands he'd had after his father's first stroke, it was only fitting that Kylie was the one to become pregnant.

Impatient with himself, he walked to the basket where they left the mail for each other, which was currently full of his grandmother's mail, and pulled the letter opener from its holder. After slitting the envelope, he was returning the opener back to the holder when a scream came from the family room.

He dropped everything and ran back there. "Charlotte, what is it?" He scooped up his crying, screaming daughter and checked for bruises. "Sunshine, can you tell me where you hurt?"

His heartbeat raced faster than a Kentucky Derby winner as he tried to figure out what was wrong. "Shh, it's okay. Tell daddy what's wrong."

His daughter started to sniff then turned her head to look over his arm. He moved in that direction, and she pointed. "Teddy."

Looking across the room, he spotted her cowboy teddy bear in the cold fireplace. He almost collapsed with relief. "You want your teddy?"

Charlotte sniffed. "Teddy."

"Daddy will get your teddy." Slowly, he lowered her back into the playpen, not willing to risk her getting over the barricade of furniture they erected to keep her out of the fireplace. Walking over, he picked up the soot-covered stuffed animal.

"Teddy?" Charlotte stood watching him, her hand out, her chubby cheeks red from crying, her little forehead crinkled with concern.

"Daddy needs to give the teddy a bath."

Charlotte shook her head. "Teddy!" She reached one hand up.

He strode across the hall into the kitchen to clean up the stuffed animal.

"Teddy! Da-da. Teddy!" Charlotte's yelling was reassuring after the blood curdling scream she'd made before.

Still, he quickly washed and rinsed it well. Grabbing up a

clean dish towel, he wrapped the teddy and brought it back to the family room.

"Teddy." His daughter laughed uncertainly through her tears.

"Yes, I need to dry him after his bath, just like I dry you."

"Dry?" She frowned then reached up one hand. "Mine. Me dry teddy."

Having sopped up the worst of the wetness, he handed Charlotte the towel and the teddy. She immediately sat down and wrapped the teddy as best she could before sticking its ear in her mouth.

Logan sank down on the ottoman to catch his breath. Crap, she'd just taken three years off his life if not more.

"Hello? Anyone here? The cowboy named Dillon said to come in. There's a storm coming up fast. It's getting pretty dark and windy out there."

He cringed at Kylie's voice. Her heels on the floor as she closed the door and stopped told him she was expecting an answer. "We're in here." He tensed, waiting for the click, click to start again.

Dammit. He hadn't opened the results yet. As he stood, she started down the hall.

"Oh, there you are. I'm so glad you're home. I wasn't sure if you'd be back yet, but I decided to take a chance since I had today off."

It had to be nearly five. Why did she wait so long? Not that he was complaining. "As you can see, I'm here."

"Good because I did some investigating, and I found out that if we file tomorrow, we can get married in Peoria by next week."

He froze. "Married?"

She smiled shyly. "I told you that in my letter, remember. You didn't say 'no,' so I went ahead and got the paperwork."

159

He stepped back. "I can't marry you, Kylie."

She lowered her eyebrows. "Why not?" She looked over at Charlotte. "I thought we were going to be a family."

"No, we're not. Charlotte and I are already part of a family. I've talked to my lawyer, and I don't think you should be part of Charlotte's life."

She wrinkled up her nose as if she'd smelled something bad. "You can't do that. I'm her mother."

Damn. Maybe talking about this with her wasn't the best thing. He should let his lawyer do the talking like he suggested. "Maybe we can work something out."

Her face brightened. "You're right, like me becoming your wife." Before he could speak, she continued. "Oh, I don't mean right now. I can see I got a little carried away. But maybe after we get to know each other better." She winked. "A lot better than just one night."

"I'm—"

The front door slammed open and banged against the door stop.

"What the…" He ran into the hall and stilled as the monsoon in the distance blocked out all the desert beyond the ranch. "Crap."

He turned back to Kylie. "Stay here with Charlotte. I have to secure the house."

At her nod, he ran to the front to make sure Dillon and Trace were bringing the horses in. Once sure of that, he passed by the family room. Kylie sat on the ottoman talking to Charlotte, who was too involved with her teddy to care.

With no other choice, he headed to the back screened-in porch and started closing windows. Latching the screen door, he finally moved inside and locked the back door.

The front door opened again and Trace and Dillon

stomped in, already spotted with the first raindrops. Trace grinned. "Everything is locked up tight. Now we just have to hope that Cyclone doesn't decide to throw a party in the barn."

Dillon closed the door. "Why is that woman leaving. Doesn't she know it's safer inside than in a car?"

"What woman?" Logan walked toward the family room wondering if it could be Kylie.

"The one in the red convertible. She didn't even lift the cover. She's going to be soaked in no time."

Logan stepped into the family room and froze, his mind trying to comprehend what he was seeing. "Charlotte!" The playpen was empty. "Where's Charlotte?"

"Brother, if you keep shouting like that, and she's hiding, she'll never come out."

He turned on Trace. "My daughter doesn't know how to hide."

"Shit, did that woman take her?" Dillon's question made him sick to his stomach.

He stalked down the hall and grabbed the results envelope. Nothing was in it. "She's got my daughter!" Without another thought, he grabbed the keys to his truck and ran outside, the pelting wind and rain soaking him completely by time he jumped in to the cab.

Within seconds he was racing down the dirt road. If she made the highway before he caught up to her, he'd lose Charlotte forever.

He now knew the answer to his grandmother's question—*what possible reason would a stranger have for finding where you live to be a mother to your daughter?* And it was closer to a crime movie plot than he was willing to go.

Jenna pulled off the highway onto the shoulder along with

161

everyone else. The monsoon had rolled in at record speed and there was no way she'd find the turnoff in the downpour. She couldn't even see the sides of the road.

As she sat there waiting for it to let up, she thought over all the different ways she could convince Logan to let Charlotte know her mother. Her plan B was to ask him if it was acceptable that they disagree on the subject since their own childhoods were so different. She wasn't going to talk to him as if he'd just dumped her because technically, he didn't.

She took a moment every couple minutes to lean down and give Butterball a reassuring pat. The poor baby was huddle in a ball on the floor on the passenger side. If he had stayed on the old bench seat, she could have cuddled him, but at the first roll of thunder, he'd leapt down and curled up.

The cars in front of her turned on their lights and one by one started to move back onto the highway. Glancing in her rearview mirror, she could see the storm moving westward, hiding the two mountains not a half mile behind her. The great thing about the monsoons is they went through pretty quickly. The bad thing was they dumped so much water that flooding happened in seconds.

Oh, fudge. There was a wash on the dirt road to the ranch. It was probably filling even as she sat there. She should probably forget it and go home, but as the rain slowed to an occasional drop, the sunset was released and the bright yellow hues were overlaid with oranges and reds. She had always thought Arizona had the prettiest sunsets.

"It's okay, sweetie. The storm is gone."

Butterball continued to huddle on the floor.

There wasn't much she could do but bring him home where he felt safe. The problem with that idea is the monsoon was headed over her house. She might as well see if the road to

Last Chance was passable. She was in a truck instead of a car, so she did have a little higher clearance.

Luckily, the Carefree Highway wasn't a very busy road out this far and she quickly pulled back onto it and headed east. She was glad she'd stopped when she did because the turn off was only a mile away.

She was more confident than ever that she and Logan could talk out this sticking point. It was important that they do or any future relationship wouldn't work. Unlike him, she wasn't about to give up at the first impasse.

"What the heck?" She stared at the sight ahead of her on the dirt road. It looked like a car was stuck in the wash she'd been worried about. As she came closer, she frowned. "Kylie?" The rushing water pushed the tiny car to the side of the road against a small hill that bordered the wash, but the woman was smack in the middle of it and the water was rising.

Kylie spotted her and waved, yelling something.

Jenna carefully drove the truck as close as she dared and rolled down the driver's side window. The sound of the turbulent water made it difficult to be heard, so she shouted. "Let me call for help!"

"No, you have to help me. I have the baby!"

The baby? What ba—Holy freak! Charlotte! "Hang on, I'm going to try and get closer!"

"Hurry!"

This had to be the stupidest thing she's ever tried to do. This is what first responders were paid to do. They were well trained. She wasn't. She started to inch forward, but the water was high and she was afraid her engine would stall and neither of them would get out.

Reversing, she heard Kylie's panicked scream.

It pulled at her heart, but she ignored it and turned around, backing down the slope closer to Kylie and Charlotte. She couldn't see Charlotte and she prayed the woman had her in a car seat or something. When she was as close as she dared, she kept the engine running and put it into park.

Now came the hard part. She climbed out her window and jumped into the bed of the truck, which was partially submerged.

"I can't reach you!" Kylie screamed over the rushing water.

Jenna pulled the rope she'd used on the breeched calf that morning and prayed it was long enough. Inching toward her tailgate, she slipped and banged against it. "Where's Charlotte?"

Kylie bent over and picked up the crying toddler, her clothes dripping.

For the first time in her life, Jenna knew pure rage. She gripped the rope hard to keep from losing complete control. She had to stay cool or none of them would get out alive. She held up the rope for Kylie to see. "Wrap this around your waist and climb out on to the front of your car!"

Kylie looked ready to balk, but as she made to put Charlotte down in the water filled car, Jenna lost it. "Stop! I have a better idea!"

At the moment, she didn't give a burrow's ass if the woman made it. Feeling under the cold water in the truck bed, she tied one end of the rope to the hook made for tying down cargo. The truck was old, but it hadn't failed her yet. She tied the other end of the rope around her waist.

In the distance, she saw movement and sincerely hoped she'd have help with all this, but she couldn't risk waiting. "I'm coming over. Be ready to grab my hand!"

Already wet up to her shins, she climbed over the tailgate and stood on the bumper. Taking a deep breath, she jumped. As she landed, she felt the car hood buckle and she reached out her hand.

Kylie grabbed it, and she made it onto the seat of the car to stand next to the woman, but the water was deep and she was short. "Give me the baby."

Kylie handed Charlotte over and Jenna once again squelched her rage at the baby's blue lips. Hugging the girl close to share her body warmth, she looked at Kylie. "I'm going to stand here and anchor the line while you walk across to my truck."

Kylie, who was now shaking with cold herself, simply nodded.

Jenna braced herself as best she could while holding the shivering Charlotte. When Kylie slipped on the hood of her car and almost went under, Jenna tensed. She couldn't save Charlotte without her.

Kylie finally found her footing and jumped to the truck. "I made it! Oh, look! They're coming!"

Jenna was growing too cold to react. "Good, now stand at the edge of the truck and I'll hand you the baby!"

Kylie did as she was told, but her gaze kept shifting to whoever approached.

Now came the hard part. With one hand, Jenna loosened the rope from around her waist and tied it to the rearview mirror, the only part of the car above water now. She just hoped the truck kept running. The bubbles from the tailpipe said it was.

Carefully, she held onto the rope and inched onto the hood of the car. The problem was, she couldn't see where it ended anymore with all the rushing muddy water. When she got as far as she dared, she yelled. "Lean over!"

Kylie did and Jenna held the baby out, but she wasn't quite close enough.

"I can't reach her!"

Grasping the child to her once again, she inched out until

she felt the hood drop off under her searching foot. Keeping the rope under her arm, she reached out with the baby again.

"Got her!"

Her relief was short lived as her feet slipped out from under her and she went down, the rope her only life line as the water covered her head.

Logan took in the scene ahead in an instant. The truck skidded to a halt just before he opened the door and ran to the wash.

Kylie held his daughter and every instinct in him told him to go to her, but he'd seen Jenna go down. He watched for what seemed minutes, until her head came up and she gasped in air.

Without hesitation, he walked into the swirling mess. Holding the side of Kylie's car until he finally lost bottom. The water was freezing cold against the hot evening and he couldn't imagine Jenna lasting long. He swam to the front of the car and caught her just as she started to go under again. "I've got you."

She glanced at him, but didn't say anything.

Fuck. His ribs burned with pain, crippling him, so he grabbed the rope. It broke loose from Kylie's car with his weight and swept them against the hill. The water and debris stung as it pressed Jenna into his ribs.

He looked at Kylie to make sure she still had his daughter. She held her close. She damn well better not get used to that.

With Jenna against him, his hand on the rope and his feet still not gaining any purchase, he looked at the hill. Maybe if he could turn toward it.

A rope hit him on the head and he looked over his shoulder. Trace sat bareback on Cyclone, a lasso in his hand. "Thought you could use some real muscle."

He ignored the comment. "Throw it again."

This time, he let go of the other rope and grabbed Trace's. As Trace started to back up Cyclone, Logan yelled. "No! That way!" He nodded toward Kylie.

Trace raised his brows but didn't say anything. Instead, he inched Cyclone into the water. Once the strong horse swam across the deepest part, Logan felt the tug and held on tight. When his feet could touch the ground, his legs didn't want to move and buckled under him.

As soon as he was pulled onto the road, he let Jenna go and yelled at Trace. "Get her into the cab and crank the heat."

Trace took Jenna away and Logan looked up at Kylie on the bed of the truck. "My daughter!"

She leaned over at his command and delivered Charlotte to him.

Charlotte eyes were open, but her lips were blue. "Da-da."

He grasped her to him, tears filling his eyes and falling onto her head. She squirmed against his tight hold, and he let her lift her face.

"Horzie!"

"Yes, that's a big—what the hell?"

Cyclone's big nose sniffed at Charlotte. At the sound of her giggle, his whole world righted itself.

"Move over, big guy. You did great!" Trace shouldered the horse out of the way and crouched down. "We need to get her in the cab. Let me take her to Jenna then we'll get you inside, too."

Reluctantly, he let his brother take his daughter to the woman he loved and almost lost. If it hadn't been for her, he would have lost his daughter as well. He swallowed the huge lump in his throat with difficulty.

The sound of sirens surprised him, and he looked around to find his cousin smiling from across the wash. Dillon raised his phone in salute. There was definitely something to be said for family.

"Okay, your turn. Ready?" Trace bent over him. With a lot of help, he maneuvered his legs under him and rose. Ironically, his ribs didn't hurt anymore, probably because they were numbed with cold. Trace opened the truck door and hot air hit him hard.

It was too tempting to ignore and he climbed in, sliding across the seat next to Jenna, who held his daughter in her arms. He pulled her against him as he carefully moved his feet next to Butterball.

Trace jumped in next to him and pulled the truck forward. "It's way too hot in here for me. I'll keep an eye on our kidnapper."

"She's going to be okay." Jenna pulled his attention as soon as the door closed on Trace.

He gazed at her, letting everything he felt for her show in his eyes. "Thanks to you. Thanks to you I now have two reasons to live."

"Really?" Hope shone in her blue-green eyes, making him want to lose himself in them.

"Yes, really. I love you, Jenna. Come here." He used his good arm to pull her closer and her lips met his before she could respond.

"Kissie. Da-da, me kissie."

Jenna laughed, breaking away. "Yes, daddy. Charlotte deserves a kissie, too. She loves you as much as I do."

He caught her soft gaze and his heart swelled. Lowering his head, he gave his daughter a big smack on the cheek. As she giggled, he looked back at Jenna.

He was the luckiest man in the world.

Epilogue

Today was the day. Jenna checked her teal button-down shirt for the fifth time, tugging it to straighten out any wrinkles. She didn't have a full- length mirror, so she hoped her black jeans fit okay.

She looked over her shoulder. "How's it look back there, BB?"

Butterball smiled up at her and wagged his tail, so he must approve. Either that or he had gas.

The sound of the dog farting filled her bedroom. Guess that answered that question. Before the smell could kill her, she grabbed up her black straw cowboy hat and exited the room. The sound of Butterball's nails hitting the wood floor behind her made it clear he wasn't happy with the stink either.

It had been a few days since she, Logan, and Charlotte had been rushed off to the hospital. They had kept Charlotte overnight for observation. She'd wanted to stay with Logan, but he forced he to go home, making Trace drive her.

She hadn't seen him since then, but he'd kept her updated via phone. Charlotte was released two days ago. The same day she released Snowy from her care, making sure Mrs. Thompson understood the kitty was on borrowed time. When she asked if Jenna liked the card, she had to admit she hadn't opened it yet.

She brought it home that day, but where did she put it? She should open it now while she nervously waited for Logan to pick her up. When he asked her to go to the jail with him to meet with Kylie, she'd been thrilled, but they still had unfinished business to discuss.

Shuffling through the mail she'd left on her kitchen table, she found the card. It was in a purple envelope and had a rose scent to it just like Mrs. Thompson. On the front of the card was a picture of a bouquet of roses and the words "Thank you." She opened it up and a check fell on to the table. It couldn't be the bill payment because they hadn't tallied it up yet. Confused, she picked up the check. "Holy fudge."

It was made out to her for $10,000 dollars. She couldn't accept that. She opened the card again and read the note. *Because you believed when no one else did. You deserve this.* Below the card's written thank you greeting was a post script. *Don't even think about not accepting this.*

But she couldn't accept it. It was one thing for a grateful rancher to throw an extra $100 her way, but this was too much. She slipped the check back into the card when she noticed something written in the memo section. *I have plenty more where that came from.*

She laughed. She still didn't plan to accept it, but it was tempting. With that kind of money, she could put a down payment on a new truck and have payments she could afford. No, she couldn't. But what if she upset Mrs. Thompson? Darn it. She'd ask Connie what she should do. That woman knew the pulse of the town. The last thing she needed was people not coming to her because she made someone angry. She tucked the check and card into her medical bag to bring to the office.

Butterball barked and waddled toward the door. She glanced out the window to see Logan's truck pulling to a stop. "Okay BB, you need to go out and do your business because I'm leaving you home alone this evening. Think you can handle that?"

He plopped his butt down in front of the door, wagged his tail and barked. "Yes, you can go out, but you'll need to stay in tonight. I don't want you struggling to breathe out there." Opening the door, her dog pulled his butt up and lumbered outside, first stopping to greet Logan before disappearing around the corner.

She caught her breath as Logan strode toward the door wearing black jeans but sporting a blue dress shirt that made his shoulders look broader and brought out the blue in his hazel eyes.

"Hi." He took off his cowboy hat and stepped in. "Are you ready?"

She closed the door and faced him, not sure exactly how to start. "I—"

Logan cupped the back of her head and kissed her, his tongue exploring her mouth like he'd forgotten what she tasted like.

He tasted of mint and male and she loved it. A light, clean-scented cologne washed over her and she practically purred.

When he released her mouth, he leaned his forehead against hers. "I missed you."

She laid her left hand on the right side of his waist. "I missed you, too."

He stood straight and pulled her against him. Though he no longer wore the sling, she knew he was still healing. They stood for a few moments, just holding each other and it felt wonderful. So much so, that it made her more reluctant to broach the subject of their last quarrel.

She finally forced herself to move back a little and look up at him. "Logan, we need to talk."

He groaned. "I'm learning to hate those words."

She cocked her head. "Why? You don't like talking?"

He raised an eyebrow. "I'm better with doing."

She nodded and stepped away before she was tempted to ask him to do exactly what his gaze promised he wanted to do. "I know you don't agree with me about Charlotte being allowed to know her mother, but your dismissal of me because of it is not acceptable."

"But that's a non-issue. We now know that Kylie isn't Charlotte's mother. She's some blood relation which is why we are going to see her."

She rolled her eyes at him. "First, since Kylie is a blood relative, that means she knows where Charlotte's mother is. Second, just because she didn't turn out to be Charlotte's mother, doesn't mean we have nothing to discuss."

He leaned his good shoulder against the wall. "Right. So talk."

He was not going to make this easy. "Since Kylie knows where Charlotte's mother is and since said mother may show up on your doorstep someday, we need to discuss the real possibility of Charlotte wanting to know her mother."

"If that day happens, I'll decide whether the woman is an appropriate influence for my daughter. Next."

She shook her head. "Logan, it's not that simple." He opened his mouth and she held up her hand. "No, it isn't. What you propose is exactly what my father did to me and my sister."

She had his attention now. Maybe her decision to share this piece of her past was the right approach. She never talked about it, but if it helped her future, she had to. "My mom lived here." She gestured to the right which led to the kitchen and living room. "We were a happy family until I turned seven. I don't even remember what time of year it was, but I know it wasn't scorching hot. My dad sent my mother away."

She tried to gather her thoughts to keep them logical and on topic, but the subject hurt, especially because her mom could well be out there somewhere and her father refused to tell her anything. That hurt on a whole other level.

Logan remained silent, watching her.

She took a deep breath. "To this day, I don't know what my mother did to deserve being thrown out, but I do know that I was devastated. She used to brush my hair, tell me stories, help me choose my clothes, play dolls with me. But then one day my dad decided she didn't deserve to be in my life anymore. As you put it, she was a bad influence."

Jenna couldn't look at Logan without tears forming so she stared at the front door. She had to get through this. "I didn't just miss her. It felt like a piece of my heart was torn out and buried in the desert somewhere. Every little-girl moment was tarnished by the fact I didn't have my mom to share it with."

She took a deep breath to loosen her tightening chest as the memories flooded her with heartache. "I avoided my prom because my mom couldn't help me pick out my dress or see me in it. When I won an award or a good grade, I could only tell my dad. I actually envied my classmates who had divorced parents because not only did they have two parents to talk to and share with, but many had four since their parents remarried other people. Some of my classmates had questionable moms, but they had one. I didn't."

She finally looked at him. "That's why I feel like I do. That's why I think that Charlotte should be allowed to know her mother. It had nothing to do with supporting you or not supporting you. We are two different people with two difference life experiences and we need to accept that we won't always agree. That doesn't mean we love each other any less."

Logan pulled away from the wall and grasped her by the shoulders. "I'm sorry. I didn't know. I was so caught up in my own self-pity that I couldn't see. Even now, when you wanted to discuss this, I was still so sure I could have it my way and only my way." He moved his hand to her cheek and brushed his thumb across it. "I do know that I'll probably do it again if we disagree, but don't let me. Promise me you won't let me push you away."

Darn. She hadn't expected that. "I promise."

He smiled. "I was going to wait to give you this when we returned, but, well, I'd like you to have it now." He held out an envelope.

Oh, she hoped he wasn't giving her money, too. That would make everything awkward. Hesitantly, she opened the envelope. There were two pieces of paper folded separately. Slowly, she opened the first one and stared at the computer generated medical terms.

She looked at him in confusion. "These are your STD and HIV results. I'm very happy that they are all negative, but why are you giving them to me?"

"You told me outside the Black Mustang that you would only consider a relationship with me if I got tested and proved to you I don't carry any sexual diseases and if I wrote down what I wanted from you."

Her heart lurched into her throat. She'd said that in anger and their relationship had changed significantly since then. She cleared her throat but her voice still came out scratchy. "I'm not sure—"

"Please. Open it."

She tried to read his face, but she could only tell one thing.

He was tense about what was in the note. "Okay." She pulled out the second piece of paper and unfolded it.

WILL YOU MARRY ME?

She snapped her head up in shock, only to find him bending one knee to kneel as he held out an open jewelry box with a simple solitaire diamond ring shining against white satin.

"Oh, my God. Are you sure?"

He chuckled. "What do you think?"

She stared into his eyes, which seemed to dance with mirth.

"Come on, Jenna. Please say you'll make me the happiest man on Earth."

Joy burst within her and she nodded, her eyes filling with tears. "Yes. Oh yes!"

Logan jumped up with a shout and hugged her tight, lifting her off her feet. "Ouch." He put her down quickly. "Damn ribs."

She smiled though her tears. "That's okay, I needed to breathe anyway."

"Let me have your hand."

She gave him her left hand and watched as he slid the ring onto her finger. "It's beautiful. It's exactly my style."

He straightened. "That's what I thought. I've always liked that you are straight forward. This reminded me of you."

She'd grown up thinking she wasn't girly enough, but if he liked her the way she was, she wasn't going to complain. "I love you, Logan."

"I love you, too. Now give me a kiss, Miss Fiancé."

As his lips touched hers, she wrapped her arms around his neck and put all that she felt for him in her kiss. In turn, he made her feel cherished and loved.

A bark from outside reminded her of their appointment. She broke away. "I guess we have to go, huh?"

He kept his arms around her. "Yes, but at least now we get to go as an official couple."

"I like that." She couldn't stop looking at him, his love for her shining in his eyes.

Another bark sounded outside, and she grimaced. "I better let Butterball in, so we can go."

He finally dropped his arms and stepped back. "Yes, or I'm apt to pick you up and carry you to your bedroom." He looked both right and left. "Wherever it is."

She chuckled as she pulled the door open and Butterball trotted inside. "Don't you want to know?"

He donned his cowboy hat. "That's something I plan to have figured out by tomorrow morning. Now let's get this over with." He held his arm out for her and she walked out, her step lighter than it had been in years.

~~*~~

"Okay, I don't want to spoil our celebration or our dinner with the full story, so let's get this over with." Gram set her oven mitts on the counter and crossed her arms over her chest.

Logan didn't dare grin. It was so like his grandmother to take charge.

Jenna elbowed him in his right side. "That means you're on."

He raised his eyebrows at her to show her he was well aware of that fact. Standing, he looked at everyone around the table, which was his grandmother, Trace and Whisper, Cole and Lacey, Dillon, Jenna and the center of the story, his daughter. "I can tell you that Kylie isn't the psycho criminal we all feared. In fact,—," he looked at his daughter for a moment before returning to his announcement. "She's Charlotte's aunt."

Dillon frowned. "With a relative like that, who needs enemies?"

Everyone nodded including Whisper. "Relatives are the worst enemies. Will Charlotte be in danger from this woman again?"

Trace took Whisper's hand. "Not all relatives are like yours."

Logan nodded at Trace's statement since he'd met Whisper's relatives and understood her concern. "Kylie is not a real criminal. That's why she didn't drive away in Whisper's truck with Charlotte when she had the chance. She stayed to help Jenna."

Jenna spoke up. "Kylie was able to tell us about Justine, Charlotte's mom."

Everyone at the table stilled.

Logan continued. "As it turns out, I was a last fling, so to speak, for Justine. Her doctor suspected she had cancer so he took a biopsy. Scared and lonely, she went to Jed's bar in Catalina where she met me. Kylie said Justine wanted to feel alive by having a fun time, just in case the biopsy came back positive. So she came on to me, and back then I wasn't about to look a gift horse in the mouth. Charlotte was conceived that night."

Logan cracked the knuckles on his left hand.

"Logan Williams, stop that."

He froze at his grandmother's words and dropped his hands. "Sorry. It's an odd feeling to know that I was the second to last joy a woman had."

Jenna's hand found his, and he squeezed. She was his rock at the jail as he learned of Charlotte's mother's fate and she was his rock now.

"Justine was told she had cancer just days later and was offered a number of options for treatment. It took her a while to decide and when she did, she was asked if she was pregnant. Kylie says her sister couldn't say for sure she wasn't so the hospital made her take a test. When she discovered she was pregnant, she refused all therapies. She wanted to deliver a healthy baby before starting any treatment."

Jenna addressed them all. "Charlotte was born perfect, but the cancer had spread in Justine."

He looked at his daughter again as she munched on a cracker. "Justine nursed Charlotte as long as she could then told Kylie to leave the baby with me because she said she was confidant I would take care of her." Logan swallowed against the lump in his throat. The reality was still too new to not be affected by it.

Jenna stood up next to him and held his arm with both her hands. "When Kylie found herself out of a job, and an illegal one at that, she decided to pose as Charlotte's mom and get Logan to marry her because if he could provide for a baby, she figured he could provide for a wife."

"Where was she going then when she took Charlotte?" Cole's question was one they had asked her directly.

Logan faced his cousin. "That was actually my fault. I told Kylie that I wouldn't marry her and that I had retained a lawyer. She panicked because she had seen the DNA test results in the hall. She knew what they said without looking at them, so she took them and Charlotte in the hopes I would give chase. She planned to go to Las Vegas where she expected to seduce me into eloping with her."

Trace laughed at the absurdity while Cole just shook his head. Lacey sighed. "I'm sorry that little Charlotte won't know her mother. I guess that means the rest of us women will just have to make up for it."

Logan's heart filled as every woman at the table agreed.

"I'll teach her to shoot." Whisper's statement caught him off guard.

"I'll teach her to ride." Gram said it like it would be law.

Lacey clapped her hands. "I'll help her pick out which clothes to buy."

The excitement was catchy and soon they were all talking about how they would be part of his daughter's life. He sank down in his seat, overwhelmed by the support.

Jenna leaned in to him and whispered. "I'll love her like she was my own."

At her declaration, he pulled his arm away and wrapped it around her shoulders, but couldn't look at her. If he did, he'd start bawling like a baby.

"Kissie, da-da! Kissie!" Ah, his daughter to the rescue.

He leaned toward Charlotte and gave her a big kiss on the cheek. She squealed then banged on her tray.

His grandmother took that as a sign to start dinner and they were soon enjoying her Mexican spiced pork ribs. Amongst the talking and laughter, he was constantly aware of Jenna next to him.

After finishing off three homemade chocolate chip cookies, he rose and lifted his daughter out of her high chair.

"Teddy." She frantically looked over his shoulder as she reached behind him. "Da-da, teddy!"

He turned around and took the cowboy teddy off the shelf and handed it to her. Her anxious face quickly relaxed into a big smile as she clutched it to her chest. He turned back to the table and offered his hand to Jenna. "Come walk with me."

She smiled up at him and took his hand, filling his heart with peace. He led her through the house and outside. As they passed the north corral, Cyclone snorted and trotted over.

Jenna stopped and waited for him to approach. When he reached the fence, he lowered his head and butted her shoulder. "Hey, big guy. Are you liking your new home? Pretty sweet deal, isn't?"

The horse stepped closer, letting her stroke his neck.

"He really likes you." Charlotte kept silent as the large head lifted over the fence. He didn't blame her since just the horse's head was bigger than she was.

"I like him, too. I would love to ride him. We're you able to use him with a harness?"

"You ride?"

She rolled her eyes. "Of course, I ride. My sister and I each had a horse growing up. That's what the barn was for. Sugar, my sister's horse, died young, but Spice reached twenty-two. He was hard to lose because I knew enough about veterinary medicine to know there was nothing I could do."

Logan moved to Cyclone's other side and patted the horse to show Charlotte there was nothing to be afraid of. "We were able to put a harness on him with no problems. He enjoyed pulling the wagon. Maybe after my ribs heal, we can take him out for a ride. I'm sure Black Jack wouldn't mind."

She stopped patting the horse and gave him a heart-stopping smile. "I would love that. I haven't ridden in years. It's hard to believe because I'm around them so much, but it's always for medical reasons, not for pleasure."

His gut did a summersault at the look of happiness on her face. He would ask Cole if he could give Cyclone to Jenna. She may be small, but he had a feeling she and the big horse were made for each other. "Then we'll plan on it."

"Mine horzie. Mine horzie, da-da." Charlotte swung her arm out toward the south corral, her cowboy teddy flailing in the evening air.

Jenna laughed. "Sorry, Cyclone. We need to go say hi to some of your friends." She patted the horse one last time and walked toward the south corral.

Logan grinned. Cyclone followed Jenna along his side of

the fence until she had gone beyond the corral. There he stood watching her. Logan set his daughter down on her feet and held her hands.

She took her little steps with gusto. Jenna turned to see where they were and immediately crouched down. "Look, Charlotte. It's your horsey." She pointed to the pony standing next to Macy.

The Sonoran desert sky was splashing oranges and pinks over the earth, giving everything a warm glow. Jenna, in particular, seemed especially beautiful to him. Maybe it was the shirt she wore that matched her eyes. Or maybe he was just seeing everything through rose colored glasses tonight.

His daughter started pulling him forward, so he let go to see what would happen. She took one step on her own and fell back on her bottom. He sighed. It would happen one day. He started to bend over to pick her up when she pushed herself up to a standing position again.

He stared in surprise.

"Want to see your horsey?" Jenna's voice was encouraging.

Charlotte continued to stand unsteadily. She lifted her hand and opened and closed it. "Mine horzie."

"Yes, he's your horsey. Come see him."

Logan held his breath as Charlotte took a step and remained upright. Then she took another. She took one more step, teetered and fell back on her bottom.

Logan swooped her up into his arms. "Good girl! You walked!"

Charlotte smiled, but was far more interested in her horse and stretched her hand out toward the corral where Jenna now stood, her eyes misty with excitement.

He strode toward his soon-to-be wife, his daughter in his arm and happiness filling his soul. When they stood next to

Jenna, he pulled his gaze from hers and spoke to his daughter. "Where's Charlotte's Horse?"

"You can't keep calling him Charlotte's Horse. It sounds like a children's story."

He frowned. "It does?"

Jenna shook her head in disbelief. "For girls and boys who actually read, yes. Have you given any thought to his name?"

He set his daughter's diapered rump on top of the fence rail, his good arm wrapped around her. She looked like a little farmer in her purple overalls. "I'm going to let Charlotte name him."

Jenna's eyes softened at his statement. She was the first one to appreciate his sentiment and that made it worth all the ribbing he'd received from his brother and cousins over the last week.

"Horzie!" Charlotte's yell caught the colt's attention and he looked over.

Logan clicked his tongue and the little horse moved toward them hesitantly to investigate.

Charlotte looked back at him, a huge smile on her face.

He bent his head to whisper. "Shh, you don't want to scare him."

His daughter pressed her finger against her lips and blew. Jenna covered her mouth to stop the laugh Logan was sure would have escaped.

He clicked his tongue again, and the colt's curiosity got the best of him. He stepped close. His tongue flicked out and licked Charlotte's shoe. The expression of wonder on her face as she snapped her head around to look at Logan made his throat close.

She turned back to the colt and the two stared at each other.

Jenna's soft voice caught the attention of both. "Charlotte, this little horsey was very lucky he had your daddy helping him when he was born."

"I think he was more lucky you were there."

"Lucky horzie." Charlotte smiled. "Mine Lucky."

Logan chuckled despite the twinge in his side. "I think she just named the horse."

"She did?"

"Yes. His name is now Lucky. Thank you for helping her."

She stepped up next to him. "I look forward to helping her with everything a little girl needs from her mother."

"How about me? I have needs to. Like right now I need a kiss."

She moved around him to his left side and stepped up onto the bottom rail.

He wrapped his arm about her loosely as she kissed him. In that simple kiss was a promise of forever.

His luck had most definitely changed.

For updates, sneak peeks, and special prizes, sign up to receive the latest news from Lexi http://bit.ly/LexiUpdate

Read on for an excerpt of Cowboy's Match (Poker Flat #2) Cole and Lacey's story

Chapter One

Cole Hatcher ignored the yellow and orange streaks of the Arizona sunset and focused on the same colors rising from the burning building as flames moved with the breeze. He spoke into the radio. "Move the two and a half inch to the northwest corner."

Two firefighters lugged the hose toward the base of the fire at the edge of the partially constructed building. Not more than fifteen feet away was a pile of old barn wood just waiting to ignite.

Stepping back toward the engine, Cole received a nod from Mason, the fire engine monitor, before speaking into the radio again. "Tanker, is the dry hydrant hooked yet?"

"Almost." The reply was not the answer Cole wanted. They would need more water than an engine and tanker could provide, and the chance of the winds picking up once the sun disappeared were better than a horse getting loose through an open gate.

As if on cue, the whinny of several frightened horses in the nearby barn caused him to tense. There was no way he would let the fire spread that way.

The radio clicked before a firefighter's voice came through. "We're hooked."

Cole breathed easier. As long as he had water, he could put this baby out. "Good. Stay with the tanker. I'll need someone to come over here and grab the one and a half inch with Clark." He watched as Clark unwound the hose, already heading toward the construction site that hid behind the smoke and flames of the fire's onslaught.

Glancing back to where the tanker was parked thirty yards away, Cole swore. "What the hell?" Coming up the hill along the dirt road his trucks had just rolled in on, were at least a half dozen golf carts filled with naked people.

He stifled a laugh. What'd they think this was? A campfire? A Wild West show? Did they plan to make s'mores? This would be a story to tell at the firehouse for sure. Still, as with all spectators to a disaster, it wasn't safe for them to be there. He silently wished he had a radio to communicate with the owner, who had enough sense to keep the resort guests from getting any closer.

For over a year, he'd been curious about the Poker Flat Nudist Resort, but Clark had been chosen to give the fire extinguisher class to all the employees before the resort opened three months ago, and Cole had no official reason to come check it out. Fighting a fire wasn't a good way to learn about a place. Whatever this new construction was, it was toast. His concern was with the barn and the horses and which way the wind would blow next.

An explosion from the fire shook the ground as flames shot into the air. "Shit." What the hell did they have in that unfinished building? The two men with the smaller hose lost their footing and fell, but since they hadn't made it to the fire yet, they were unharmed.

He'd be damned if he'd put his men in harm's way when no lives were at stake.

He turned toward the owner and motioned her closer, then faced the burning construction site. As the sky behind the fire turned a dull pink, the breeze picked up, changing the direction of the flames toward the open desert. Good for the horses, but not for wildfire potential. It'd been the driest summer on record. October temperature highs had finally dropped below triple digits and the nights were already getting cold, but there had been no rain during monsoon season.

Cole spoke into the radio again. "I need the two and half inch to lay down a curtain between the building and the open desert on your side."

"Got it." The two firefighters adjusted their hose and started a continual spray, wetting and cooling the area toward the open desert even as the men with the one and a half inch hose moved in to cover the fire base.

"Lieutenant, you wanted us?" The female voice had him turning around.

He'd forgotten he'd called over the owner. At least she and the cowboy with her were dressed. "You need to get those people out of here. I can't control the fire's embers and right now the wind is picking up."

The tall man nodded. "I'll take care of that." He immediately strode toward the golf cart brigade.

Cole turned his attention to the woman. "I've got my men focused on keeping the fire from spreading to your barn or out into the desert. A wildfire would be catastrophic, but we won't be able to save the building."

She waved her hand as if it meant little to her. "I'm not worried about the building as long as everyone is safe."

"Have you accounted for all your employees and guests?"

"Yes."

Another explosion had Cole turning away to check on his men. A voice came across his radio. "What the fuck is in here? A chemical lab?"

Cole frowned. He'd never thought of how convenient it would be to have a meth lab out at a nudist resort. He'd make sure the police investigated the place in case there had been illegal activity.

He looked at the owner. "How many more explosions should we expect?"

She frowned. "We had one before you arrived, that's what alerted me to the fire, but there shouldn't be anything that would explode over there. The plywood for the roof was completed, but they hadn't even set the windows in yet. All that was there was whatever the construction crew left."

"Do you have electricity out there yet?"

She shook her head.

Shit. "Gasoline for their generator." He spoke into his radio again. "Possible gas containers."

A gust of wind compounded his problems and he quickly repositioned his men. A siren could barely be heard in the distance, but the red and blue lights of a sheriff department car reflected far into the desert. About time they got here.

Cole spared a glance to where the golf carts had been parked and was relieved to see only a few left, but he scowled as a young woman with golden hair moved toward him and the owner, a tray of food and drinks in her hands. Shit, didn't these people realize this was a working fire? This was dangerous!

A third explosion rocked the ground and he spun in time to see a gust of wind pick up the roiling flames and throw them toward his men. He pressed the button on his radio. "Fall back!"

One man stumbled backward, catching his foot on the old barn wood and lost his grip on the hose. The other firefighter struggled with it before he went down too.

"Fuck." Cole sprinted to his men, pulling them back by

their coats as the flames licked at their boots. The barn wood caught, feeding the fire.

Once his men were out of harm's way, he tackled the flailing line. A loose hose was a danger in its own right.

"Lieutenant, do you want us on the wood pile?" The question came through his radio.

Cole slammed his body onto the hose before replying, "Negative. Keep that curtain up."

The two firefighters that had been blown down regained their feet and grabbed the hose. "Thanks, Lieutenant."

He released his hold. "Pull back and soak that pile. If the wind shifts again, I don't want the barn catching."

The men nodded.

Cole turned around and strode back to the engine. The two women were still there. This wasn't a movie. Didn't they have any common sense?

After checking with Mason to be sure the water pressure was steady, he approached his audience, irritation growing at the petite stature of the blonde. Someone so delicate didn't belong at a working fire, but like the owner, at least she had clothes on. "Ladies, you need to get back." He pointed to the rise the golf carts had congregated on earlier.

The blonde smiled. "Selma sent over churros and iced tea for your men in case they need something."

Cole's blood froze. *That voice.* He studied the woman and his heart stumbled inside his chest. Her shapely figure proved she'd grown into a delectably curvy woman as he'd always expected she would, but her face was almost the same, just more refined. "Lacey Winters?"

Her brows furrowed and her button nose wrinkled as she peered back at him. Had he really changed so much in eight years? Yeah, probably. He'd been a bean pole last he'd seen her…the night he broke it off with her.

She gave up trying to figure out who he was. "I'm sorry. Do I know you?"

He should let it go. No need to dredge up the past. He had a fire to control.

His pulse went into overdrive. Another fire. It couldn't be coincidence. He scowled at her. "You should. I'm Cole, Cole Hatcher."

Even in the reflection of the flames, her face turned pasty white and he kicked himself for revealing his identity. All he needed now was a fainting woman to contend with.

"You two know each other?" The other woman leaned on one hip, her concern for Lacey evident in the look she gave him.

At the owner's voice, Lacey recovered her color. Actually, her face changed from white to an angry flush in a matter of seconds. It reminded him of a flashover.

"Not that I want to know him." Lacey handed the tray over to the owner and stepped up to him. She poked her index finger into his chest. Hard. "So, Cole Hatcher. Are you going to accuse me of setting this fire? After all, I'm here, on the same property. It's not like you need evidence or anything. Feel free to assume the worst. I'm sure it helps to justify the way you treated me." She pulled back as if touching him made her feel sick. "Good luck with that." Turning on her heel, she stalked off, her hips swaying enticingly until he remembered where he was and who he was looking at.

"So *you're* the one who broke her heart." The owner studied him briefly then set the tray on the ground and followed after Lacey.

Shit.

Lacey didn't have a destination in mind. She didn't even see the dirt road she walked on. All she could see was Cole Hatcher, or rather the new and improved Cole Hatcher. He'd grown even taller and had filled out like a pro football player. What right did he have to look that good?

"Lacey, wait." Kendra's voice stopped her.

She didn't want to wait. She wanted to get as far from Cole as she could. That was why she'd applied for the job at Poker Flat in the first place. But Kendra was her boss.

"Lacey." Kendra grabbed her arm. "Were you planning to walk into the ravine?"

She looked at her boss blankly before refocusing on her surroundings in the growing darkness. Shoot. She'd almost walked right off the road.

She returned her gaze to Kendra and shook her head, her eyes watering at her near miss. She shouldn't let Cole affect her so much. She was supposed to be over him by now.

Kendra looped her arm in hers. "Come on. Let's let the firefighters do their job and you can tell me all about it."

Lacey swallowed the lump in her throat. "I'd rather not."

"That wasn't a request." Kendra tugged on her arm and she gave in. Her boss was twice her size and tough. Besides, Lacey owed her an explanation. Her broken heart and arson charge had been the two deciding factors for getting hired. Kendra only hired misfits and at first Lacey had appeared too perfect.

She sniffed. Heck, she was anything but perfect.

"So he's the one who broke your heart, isn't he?" Kendra didn't waste time getting to the point.

"Yes."

"I thought you said he was a cowboy and lived in Orson, Arizona."

Lacey pulled up her memory of the young man she'd fallen head over heels for. He'd been six feet tall as a high school senior and as thin as any wrangler, but even then his hard chin had given him a more mature look. Her weakness, though, had been his eyes. Cole Hatcher had always had the kindest green eyes she'd ever gazed into.

"Lacey?"

"Yes, he is, he was, I don't know. I have no idea what he's doing here or why he's a firefighter." Her stomach tensed. The last time they were at a fire together, he held her close as her parents' carriage house went up in smoke.

Kendra steered her toward her own casita. "I think we'd better have this conversation at your place."

Lacey stopped, forcing Kendra to halt. "We can't do that. We have guests and they will all be in the main building asking questions, needing food and attention."

"Of course they will, and Wade and Selma can take care of them. You and I are going to your casita." Kendra tugged her into walking again.

She sighed. She'd finally forgotten about Cole, except for the dull ache of her bruised heart. She'd moved on, gone to college, done what was right, as she always had…except he'd ignored that fact when he decided to agree with the rest of the town.

Kendra stepped back when they reached the door to her casita.

Pulling her resort keyring from the pocket in her skirt, Lacey quickly identified her house key and unlocked the door. She flicked the light switch and a pale-yellow glow filled the living room. "Would you like some lemonade?"

Kendra hooked her arm again and steered her to her white wicker couch with the cactus floral cushions. "No, I don't want anything to drink. I want you to tell me why you and that hunk of a firefighter out there aren't living happily ever after on a ranch in Orson."

Lacey sat and clasped her hands as Kendra pulled the matching wicker chair over to sit opposite her.

"I'm not sure where to start."

"Okay, then I'll ask the questions and you answer them. How long had you two been an item?"

Technically, they had met sophomore year of high school, but it was their junior year that they became an item. "About two years."

"How long has it been since you last saw him?"

She gripped her hands tighter. "Eight years."

"And what caused the breakup?"

Lacey narrowed her eyes. "That stupid arson charge." Her tone dripped with bitterness she couldn't control. She'd always been a good girl, and being accused of something she didn't do had rankled.

"Ah, so he broke up with you because he thought you were a firebug and as a future firefighter he couldn't be with you."

"Yes. No. I mean, yes, he did believe the accusations and dumped me because he couldn't be with 'someone like me' as he so graciously put it. But he was a cowboy then, not a firefighter. He was supposed to stay in Orson and take over his parents' horse ranch."

Kendra pondered that information for a moment. "But didn't you say when I hired you that they ruled that fire as accidental?"

She shrugged. "Yes, but by the time they made that decision, I was away at school and my reputation in Orson was dirt." The fact was, she'd been lucky to escape from the burning carriage house. It had taken her over a year to get over the nightmares of waking up in the dark, her lungs filling with smoke.

Kendra stood. "I want you to stay in this casita all night. I don't want anyone trying to blame this fire on you."

"You believe me?"

Her boss rolled her eyes. "Lacey, I didn't have to work with you for a year and let you handle all my money to know you wouldn't have started a fire. The fact that some idiot who supposedly loved you couldn't figure it out doesn't mean the rest of the world is so stupid."

Tears welled in her eyes and Lacey threw her arms around Kendra. "Thank you."

Her boss gave her a tight hug, then pushed her back. "First rule, don't let him see your weakness. Got it?"

Lacey nodded and brushed her tears away with the hem of her western shirt, even though her heart was breaking all over again. Kendra had been a professional poker player and if anyone would know how to appear to Cole, it would be her.

"Second, don't give him the opportunity to point fingers. Go about your daily business as if nothing unusual has happened."

She nodded. "But what about the real reason the fire started?"

Kendra scowled. "Shit, that could be anything from more vandals hating our nudist business to a careless construction worker to a guest with an arson record. We'll let the fire department figure that out. Okay?"

"Okay." She straightened her shoulders. "I'll stay here tonight and review Selma's inventory. I have it on my computer."

Kendra walked to the door. "Good. Maybe you can also check our reservations and see if anyone is due to arrive tomorrow. I'd like to know what kind of guest relation mitigation we will be up against with the police and fire people here."

"Already did." Lacey opened the door for her boss. "No one is due to check in until Wednesday when Ginger and Buddy arrive, unless we have day guests."

Kendra smiled. "Good. That's one thing in our favor.

Ginger and Buddy won't care." Instead of turning away, her boss shifted her weight, a clear sign she was concerned.

Lacey's stomach tightened. "What is it?"

"I just realized how important it is for me to hire a new security guard. It's been so quiet this fall I haven't made time for interviews. Now with your ex in the area, I'm thinking that should become my first priority."

She was about to reassure Kendra that Cole didn't have a dangerous bone in his body, but she swallowed her words as the image of him hefting his fellow firefighters away from the flames came to mind. The teenage Cole certainly didn't have that kind of strength. Truth be told, she didn't know *this* Cole Hatcher at all.

~~*~~

Cole fell into a cushioned chair in the Poker Flat Nudist Resort's lobby and lifted the neck of his t-shirt up to wipe his eyes. The material came away dotted with tiny black specks. Shit, he needed a shower. Just a few more minutes and he could head back to the station.

Wade Johnson, the resort manager, strode away in search of his fiancée, the owner of Poker Flat. The man had stayed up all night with him. Their mutual interest in protecting the horses had Cole thinking. It may be a nudist resort but it was still a resort. He couldn't pass up a possible opportunity for the horses from his and his grandfather's ranch. He'd see if he could get a business card.

Crossing his legs at his ankles, Cole leaned back. He had to admit the resort was first class. The chair he sat in was so comfortable he'd have to be careful not to fall asleep. He glanced at the wooden clock above the receptionist desk. 5:50 a.m. He doubted many nudist guests would be up yet. He could close his eyes until Wade returned. Watching for hot spots all night to protect the desert and the horses had been a strain on the eyes.

A slight change in air temperature was the only warning he had he wasn't alone anymore.

"Oh come on, Selma. You were sitting at your kitchen table twiddling your fingers waiting for the sun to rise. Now you have an extra ten minutes to prep your huevos rancheros."

"Humph. Could have used the extra minutes for my beauty sleep."

Cole opened one eye. Lacey strode toward the front desk in a pair of white cowgirl boots with fringe, a too short white skirt, and a loose white blouse with tiny pink stars and six-shooters printed on it. The only thing missing was a white hat, except she had that too, in her hand. From behind she made him think of a piece of tres leches cake with strawberries on top. The desire to eat her up hit him in the groin.

She stopped at the desk and gave the shorter woman with salt-and-pepper hair a quick hug. "You are far too beautiful as it is."

The woman ducked away, grumbling, but Lacey smiled after her fondly. Cole's heart thumped hard in his chest. He remembered that smile. It had made him believe he could conquer the world. Too bad he hadn't had her with him when he needed to conquer his parents.

Lacey moved to adjust the pamphlets on the side of the counter. Her shapely legs had a slight tan as they disappeared beneath the ass-hugging skirt. He scowled. She shouldn't wear such revealing clothes to work. Was she looking to get laid? Her straight blonde hair was caught in a braid on one side of her neck, giving her an innocent look.

She wasn't innocent at all. As a randy teen, he'd made sure of that. Need slithered through his crotch and up his backbone.

The first time he'd had her petite body beneath his own, he'd been afraid of crushing her. But his little lady was made of sterner stuff on the inside. His balls tightened and he shifted in the chair, his erection making him uncomfortable. She'd been so tight.

"What are *you* doing here?"

Cowboy's Match (Poker Flat #2)
http://www.lexipostbooks.com/cowboys-match/

Also by Lexi Post

Contemporary Cowboy Romance

Cowboys Never Fold
(Poker Flat Series: Book 1)
Cowboy's Match
(Poker Flat Series: Book 2)
Cowboy's Best Shot
(Poker Flat Series: Book 3)
Cowboy's Break
(Poker Flat Series: Book 4)
Christmas with Angel
(Poker Flat Series Book 2.5/Last Chance Series: Book 1)
Trace's Trouble
(Last Chance Series: Book 2)
Fletcher's Flame
(Last Chance Series: Book 3)
Logan's Luck
(Last Chance Series: Book 4)
Dillon's Dare
(Last Chance Series: Book 5) *Coming 2018*

Military Romance

When Love Chimes
(Broken Valor Series: Book 1)
Poisoned Honor
(Broken Valor Series: Book 2)

Paranormal Romance

Masque
Passion's Poison
Passion of Sleepy Hollow
Heart of Frankenstein *Coming 2017*
Pleasures of Christmas Past
(A Christmas Carol Series: Book 1)
Desires of Christmas Present
(A Christmas Carol Series: Book 2)
Temptations of Christmas Future
(A Christmas Carol Series: Book 3) *Coming 2017*

Sci-fi Romance

Cruise into Eden
(The Eden Series: Book 1)
Unexpected Eden
(The Eden Series: Book 2)
Eden Discovered
(The Eden Series: Book 3)
Eden Revealed
(The Eden Series: Book 4)
Avenging Eden
(The Eden Series: Book 5) *Coming 2018*

About Lexi Post

Lexi Post is a New York Times and USA Today best-selling author of romance inspired by the classics. She spent years in higher education taking and teaching courses about the classical literature she loved. From Edgar Allan Poe's short story "The Masque of the Red Death" to Tolstoy's *War and Peace*, she's read, studied, and taught wonderful classics.

But Lexi's first love is romance novels. In an effort to marry her two first loves, she started writing romance inspired by the classics and found she loved it. From hot paranormals to sizzling cowboys to hunks from out of this world, Lexi provides a sensuous experience with a "whole lotta story."

Lexi is living her own happily ever after with her husband and her cat in Florida. She makes her own ice cream every weekend, loves bright colors, and you will never see her without a hat.

www.lexipostbooks.com